THROUGH A CHILD'S EYES

by

B. M. Bradley

BMP

Blue Mendos Publications

Published by Blue Mendos Publications
in association with Lulu Enterprises Inc.
3101 Hillsborough Street
Suite 210
Raleigh, NC 27607-5436
United States of America

Published in paperback 2016
Category: Fiction
Copyright B. M. Bradley © 2016
ISBN : 978-1-326-76005-2

Author's photograph © Jon Courtney 2016

Disclaimer

*This book is based on the author's recollection of events,
conversations and facts. The conversations are not written to
represent word-for-word transcripts. Rather, the author has retold
the events in a way that evokes the feelings and meaning of what
was said in all instances, the overall essence of the dialogue is an
accurate reflection of the author's memory. Names, places and
some identifying features have been altered and invented or
altered for literary effect.*

Dedication:

With love to the memory of a very special aunt Rita and uncle Don. The sanctuary and love they showed me as a child and also as a young adult will never be forgotten. Love you both to the stars and back xx.

Chapter One

I woke to the sound of her shoes, the heels click clacking as she walked at speed down the path. The closer she got to the house, the louder the click clacking. I lay very still, not even letting, out a breath. Then his voice was deep and muffled, I couldn't work out what he was saying. Then I heard her voice, hers was shrill and pleading, she was upset with him. The key went into the lock, a few seconds passed by and then the door banged shut. She was still pleading with him, "but I was just asking her about the ham and eggs". His voice was still muffled, probably due to the amount of alcohol he had consumed. They went out nearly every Sunday night, to the pub in the nearest town, to meet friends and drink alcohol. Some Sunday nights they would come home and be very happy, they were great friends who were conscious they had children sleeping upstairs and would try to be quiet, giggling and whispering when going upstairs to bed together. I loved those nights, the sound of laughter was not often heard in this house, so it was a cherished sound.

The lounge room door was slammed shut and the sound of angry voices faded. I felt myself exhale as the sound of their argument dispersed and I drifted back to sleep.

Then I woke again, unable to work out, how long I had been back to sleep. I heard him first, trying to run up the stairs in a clumsy way, tripping at what I guessed was the middle stairs, which sent him into a greater rage. The bedroom door was pushed open and I froze in bed, my eye lids pressed firmly shut so I did not give him any eye contact and he would see I was sleeping along with my older sister in the bed next to mine.

Then I felt the heat of pain in my head as he pulled me with my hair, from my bed. The smell of alcohol was stinging my eyes and my fear was increasing, I was sure I was going to wet myself. I had never had the best bladder control but this made me need to pee even more. I kept wishing myself not to pee. I no longer felt the pain, just heat in my head. I was now sitting up on the edge of my bed, his large hand holding my hair firmly and pulling me closer to his face. The smell of alcohol was stronger and stronger with every breath and sound he made. "Where is she? I won't say it again. I said, where is she? You better tell me now, I'm going to fucking kill her, and I've had enough of this. I know, you know where she's gone. Get up, get up and get down stairs, and into that car, you can show me where she's gone". I was crying with fear and wishing my big sister would wake up and talk to him, he would listen to her, she was his favourite. He would never harm her, pull her hair, or shout at her like this. But no she was still fast asleep in her bed, not moving or even making any sounds.

He dragged me with my hair to the door of our small bedroom, I was unable to get to my feet fast enough. He kept hold of my hair tight and pulled until I was on my feet. As he opened the door and pushed me towards the landing, he leaned and lost his grip on my hair, as he swayed into the door of their bedroom, just to the right of our bedroom. This was my opportunity to get down the stairs before he pushed me or dragged me down them. I rushed to the stairs as fast as my legs would take me and managed to stay in front of him as he followed me, stumbling and swaying down the stairs, all the time he continued to shout at me, "where has she gone, I know she told you, you're sly just like she is, tell me where she's gone, I'm warning you. If you don't tell me, god help me, I'll break your scrawny little neck, and that's exactly what she is going to get. She thinks she can make a mug of me, in front of all me mates, well, I'll show her whose the mug, mark my words".

I was standing outside the front door now, in only my night dress, it was November and I had nothing on my feet and no underwear on either. I wasn't cold, or concerned about my lack of underwear, I just wanted to know where she had gone. I wanted them to make friends and let me go back to bed. Again I started to feel like I was going to pee myself, with every breeze and cold shiver I let out a little wee. He can't catch me, he will go mad if he notices I've wet myself. But I just couldn't keep it in.

We lived at No 2, a little cul-de-sac with only 16 houses, we knew everyone in the close. I knew all the children, I had friends at number 4, 5 and 7 for most of my childhood. There were other children but they were either a lot older than me or younger than me. We would spend time playing in each other's houses, bedrooms or out on the

9

street together. Her friends and neighbours were referred to as aunts and uncles, even though they were not related, it was just how it was done then. Aunt Nora was a big lady, with two daughters and a son and they lived at number 5, I would play with the youngest daughter Lisa and my older sister would play with her older sister, Sally. My sister never wanted us to join in any of their games, she always complained if I asked to play with her and she would tell him or her and I would then be brought in and not allowed to play out anymore for bothering my older sister.

A car turned into our close, he stopped shouting at me and looked towards the car. It was a taxi, bringing one of our neighbour's home. I quickly stepped back and he walked past me, stumbling up the path towards his car. He slipped off the edge of the path into the flower bed and started to swear under his breath. He got to the other side of the gate, turned round fast and nearly missed his footing again. He just managed to stabilise himself, when he looked towards me and shouted "get in the car". I was frozen to the spot, urine slowly trickling down my legs. I was glad it was dark, or he would have seen I was making quite a puddle on the floor. I tried to reason with him. "Why don't we wait here until she comes back? I'm scared, I don't want to get into the car". I cried, my nose running and tears running down my face and still unable to stop myself for weeing. I sniffed up and then tried to wipe my nose with the sleeve of my night dress. "Where are we going? It's too dark to go out". "Where are we going she asks, it's too dark she says" in a mocking high pitched voice. "Get in the car now, I won't tell you again.

You're, going to take me to her, you know where she's gone and you better show me, NOW". I was now walking towards the rear car door. I was always told to get into the back. Lucy would get to sit in the front and the little ones were allowed in the front having tries and turns. I was never allowed in the front. "You get in the back, I can't be listening to your gob all day" He'd say, if ever I tried to get in the front seat. I was now used to just going straight to the back seat. Tonight though he shouted, "No, here", showing me to the front of the car in the passenger seat. I started to cry, no matter how much I wanted to hold it in, I could not stop the tears but at least I'd stopped peeing. The wind and cold had almost dried my legs, I was praying he would be too drunk to smell the urine on me. "Oh for Christ sake, stop your bloody whinging, I'm not putting up with you too". "But I don't want to go out in the car, Can I go back to bed now? I don't know where she is, honest". All the while he was pointing to the passenger seat and I was slowly walking towards this and then sitting on the passenger seat. He walked slowly in front of the car, swaying as he passed the front window. He sat in the car and set it off to the top of the street. I continued crying, my nose continued to run and I was also sniffing up. I then said, "Can we go home and see if Lucy knows where she is? I don't want to go out". "GET OUT, GET OUT" he yelled at me. I was shocked and unsure if I was to do as he had ordered or if I was going to get into more trouble, if I did in fact, get out of the car. He slowed the car to nearly a stop, we had only just got even with number 3, the Carter's house when he shouted again, "GET OUT, NOW". I quickly opened the car door and got out, losing my balance and falling half onto the path and on the road. My nightdress rising up and exposing me. I grazed my hip and ankle but was not aware of this at the time. I quickly got to my feet and ran back to our garden and down the path, back into the house and closed the door. I could hear his car engine revving on the close and then I think I heard the car pass our house and leave the close. I stood behind the door until I could no longer hear the sound of the car.

I relaxed, my back against the front door, and felt myself breath a loud sigh, then start to shake and cry. I walked slowly into the lounge, sank onto the chair and felt my tense and cold body start to relax. Just as I realised I had a sore area on my hip, the lounge room door opened slowly. I froze on the spot and felt myself take in a gasp of air. My sister's head appeared round the door. "Right come on, upstairs and help me". I didn't ask any questions I just followed her back upstairs to our bedroom. She shut the door and then started to push the single wooden wardrobe we shared. She pulled on one side of the wardrobe and it moved slightly away from the built-in wardrobe that was behind it. "Come on help me, I can't do this on my own" I did as I was told, I squeezed into the gap she had created between the walk in wardrobe door and wooden wardrobe. Pushing with all my weight to move the wardrobe. I didn't stop to ask why; I was used to doing as I was told. My big sister 'Lucy' was not someone I argued with. She was always irritated when I was around. She didn't like me; I knew this from a very early age. She was bigger than me, 3 years older and much prettier than me, he liked her more than any of us, and she was always his favourite. I felt like I had been pushing for what seemed like about 10 minutes, but was probably a minute or two at most. We had manage to move the wardrobe, just enough for the door to open. Lucy came to the side I was pushing from and then pulled at my night dress, "get out of the way, let her out for god's sake, and move". Then out my mother came, from the walk-in wardrobe, she squeezed herself, out between the door and wall. I stood back, still rubbing my hands from the pressure of pushing the wardrobe. "Oh no, if he comes back and finds you, he will kill you". I remember the look on her face, mascara stained below her eyes, she had been crying. Had he hit her again? I asked "how long have you been in there? Did he hurt you?" I was pushed out of the way by Lucy, "oh shut up with all your questions, he's gone out. You know that, you let him get into the car and drive away, knowing he was drunk."

Still I stood staring and listening to Lucy asking her, what the argument was over? Why was he so mad? What had she done this time to make him so angry? Not that this was any different than most Sunday nights. He would be drunk and angry no matter what was said or done.

We all headed out of the bedroom to go downstairs, one of the boys had woken up, it was Peter, sitting at the top of the stairs in a daze, he still looked half asleep. Jimmy and Luke were still sleeping in their beds. Oblivious to what had been unfolding in the other bedroom, Peter stood as we came out of the bedroom. She shouted at him, "how long have you been sitting there? Go back to bed now and get to sleep". He did as he was told and we went downstairs into the lounge. Lucy switched on the electric fire and sat on the rug in front of it. I liked the electric fire, it had bulbs with little aluminium plates that balanced and spun round when the fire was switched on and this created a firelight effect to reflect above the actual fire bars, making it look like a real log fire burning. I could sit and stare at this light for ages, it took me away from all this, into my own fantasy land, with no shouting and just happy times.

"Go make a brew, I said, are you deaf as well as stupid"? I quickly got up and left the lounge to make a cup of tea. I stood in the kitchen, trying to hear what she was talking about with Lucy, the kettle began to boil and this noise drowned out any sound of them talking. I quickly made the tea, the cold floor beneath my feet, I walked carefully and carried the mugs into the lounge. We all sat again in front of the fire, I was now left with a little space at the edge of the rug and could just feel a little of the heat. She was sitting directly in front of the fire and Lucy close by her side. We sat in silence for a few minutes, all three of us with our own thoughts. I was aware I was straining to hear any noise from the street. Could I hear his car? Will he come back tonight and if so will he come back in a better mood or will he come back angry and want to hurt her again?

Lucy got up and went to the window and pulled the curtains open to look out into the dark night. I stood, fear driving through me, I shouted "close the curtains, if he sees them open and sees this light on he will come back in". I was now getting more and more anxious and my voice seemed to be screeching and I was unable to catch my breath, I felt pain in my chest. She then stood and pushed me to the chair, "shut up, will you? You'll wake the little ones". I then curled my feet underneath me and sat curled up on the chair. Lucy closed the curtains, "it's just a taxi" she said and then walked back to sit on the rug in front of the fire. The room had now warmed up to a comfortable heat. But then I was still shivering.

"So when he comes back and asks where I was, don't forget, you tell him, I have just got in from hiding in the back garden, right? He must never know where I hide." "Oh she can't be trusted, she will blab, she always does" said Lucy. "No I don't, I won't say a thing" I protested. "Look, he must never find out, or you're right, he will kill me, If he finds out I was in the house all the time he will go mad, that reminds me the wardrobe needs putting back, Eddy, go and push the wardrobe back over the walk-in wardrobe door so he doesn't see it has moved". "But how am I supposed to do that on my own?" "Just go and do it and stop being awkward, I can't do it I'm too upset, and I'm not doing it again, go on it will only take you a minute, go on". Off I went back upstairs to push the wardrobe back. I surprised myself at how easy this seemed to be, I just pushed, stood with my back to the wardrobe and wedged my feet against Lucy's bed for leverage, then leaned into it and pushed until it would not go any further and it was back in place.

I quickly went to cover up my bed, it was still stained from last night's accident but I had gotten away with it by saying I had not wet the bed. I had been up before anyone else and quickly went to the bathroom and put my dirty nighty and knickers into the bottom of the laundry basket and then covered my bed up with the top covers. I didn't always manage to get away with this, but it did work some days. I could not face her being angry at me now, so I covered up the evidence and then went to the bathroom. I had been bursting for the toilet for some time. I was sitting daydreaming, thinking of what will happen when he comes home. Will I get to go to school in the morning? Will I be able to get my lunch money off him? I could see the lights of the cars going up and down the lane. Just one car going up, then two going down. It was around 3am now, I walked from the bathroom and started to head down the stairs. Half way down the stairs, I could see the figure of a person, tall in dark clothing, walking down the path towards the front door. I froze to the spot with four steps still to reach the bottom. I shouted "MUM, MUM". It was him, I was sure it was him, he had come back, he's going to be even more angry when he finds us all up and he is going to kill us all. The figure carried on walking getting bigger and bigger as they approached the door. Mum did not answer, I had actually imagined shouting her, but due to my fear rising, I had been able to get the words out of my mouth. The figure seemed to get wider and wider and then a knock on the door, brought me back to reality. I started to cry, "No don't let him in", a harsh sounding "Sssshhhhhh", came from the lounge room. The panic inside me increased, "No, No, Go away, don't let him in". Lucy came to the door first and mum followed her. "Shut it, I won't tell you again, you will wake the little ones". I ran past in a panic as she reached to the latch to open the door.

I was sat in the lounge at the far side on the end of the sofa, ready to drop down the side out of view. Mum then returned to the lounge followed by two police officers. The female officer walked across the room towards me and sat beside me, and the male officer sat in the chair by the lounge door. Mum walked in slowly and stood in front of the fire, hands over her mouth, "what has he done now?" she said. Lucy stood by her side, "shut up will you and let him talk" said Lucy. The male officer then began by asking questions, like "what make, model and colour car does he drive?" "It's a Blue, Ford, it's at work, and he decided to leave it at work, Friday night, as he went to the pub after work". Ok, said the male officer. Can you give a description of your husband please and tell me where he is now?" "Look, he's not here yet, he went out with his friends, he won't be long, what's he supposed to have done this time?" The female officer then leaned forward and said, "It's important we locate your husband as a matter of urgency, we have reason to believe a car owned by your husband has been involved in a serious accident and we need to identify the driver, so it's very important we get as much information from you as possible. If you know where your husband is now, could you call him on the telephone or tell us where he is and we can go to see him and confirm he is ok?"

We all let out a gasp, I stared at the police officer and Lucy started to scream and cry, through her tears she asked "is he dead? Oh no, he's dead, isn't he? See what you have done now". She stepped towards me, anger and rage on her face, what had I done? Had he actually died? The female officer stood up in front of her and very calmly said to her, "Now now, let's not get ahead of ourselves, your mum said your dad left his car at work so we don't know who it is, now do we? There has been an accident and we need to gather as much information as possible about your husband's whereabouts and the location of his car before we make any bold statements", she stood and held Lucy to her. The male officer was now talking, "I know this is a shock at this early hour of the morning, but we have reason to believe your husband may have been driving the car. Do you think he may have gone to work to collect his car to drive back home?" "Yes, yes, he could have done that, he probably didn't have anything to drink tonight and wanted to have his car for work in the morning. Has he been hit by another car? Have you got the other car? It won't be his fault, he's a good driver, he's very careful". She was lying, why was she lying? My head was starting to hurt again, why, was she lying, tell them. Tell them, he was going to kill you, he was going to kill US. Why was she lying to them, they could help us? I could not believe what I was hearing. The male officer had told us he was called Tim and he looked like a very nice man, very tall with short red hair and dark rimmed glasses. He sat on the edge of the chair holding his little black pad and pen, writing down everything she was saying. "Can you remember what clothes

18

he was wearing?" "Black jacket, black trousers and blue shirt, and a blue tie". The officer then flicked backwards through his little pad. "A blue tie you say? Could he have taken off the tie or decided not to wear it?" She looked at the male officer then at Lucy, who was now sitting on the sofa at the other side of me with the female officer in the middle. She looked at the officer, not offering any response to his question. He repeated the question, "maybe he decided to take off the tie tonight? Could that be possible?"

The police officers' radios were transmitting all the time they were in our lounge. The officers had turned the volume down on the radios, but then the female officer stood and said, "Excuse me Sarge, I'm just going to get this," he nodded and she then left the room. I could hear her speaking as she walked and talked then went to stand in the garden. She left the lounge door and the front door open, the heat from the fire was now quickly leaving the room. I then realised I was shivering, but I was not feeling cold, I could not control the shivering and shaking of my body. I could hear the radio sounds and the police officer was outside for what felt like an hour talking to the person on the other side of the radio. The female officer then came back into the lounge and asked Tim to go and speak with her, they both left the house to go into the garden and talk in hushed voices.

Mum looked over at me and Lucy and with a warning frown, she put her index finger to her mouth and mouthed, "Keep it shut", to both of us. Lucy took in a breath and was just about to respond when the officers came back into the lounge. Again they asked her to sit down, again she declined. "Just tell me, please, just tell me, what's happened to him, he better be ok, I'm telling you we have five children here. If he's been hit by another driver you better have him. I'm warning you, if anyone has hit him and you don't have them in custody, I can tell you he won't be responsible for what he does to them, he's not a man to be messed with. Believe you me". Her voice was shaky and she sounded like she was going to cry. Why is she upset? He may be dead, he can't hurt us if he is dead, is she really upset? I couldn't tell. She stood and Tim then said, "Ok, ok, we need to tell you this. Please calm down and let me speak". He said in a louder but calm manner. "We have just had confirmation from the accident site that we have one casualty and we have reason to believe, it is your husband's car, the driver of the car is the only person involved in the accident. The male driver has been taken to the local hospital. The rescue team have found the casualty has his wallet on him and this has been used to identify him as a Mr James Crawley as we believe this to be your husband". She took in a sharp breath and held her head in her hands and started to cry. Tim walked forward and placed his hand on her shoulder and asked her again to take a seat. Again she shrugged her shoulders and shook her head in a refusal to sit down. Tim went on to say, "I know this is a shock, however, we still need you to come with us to the hospital to ensure the identification is correct. Is that ok with you?" She seemed to calm down and her tears started to dry up. She looked up at the female officer and then looked around the room. Tim went on to say, "Do you have anyone

20

you can ask to can come and stay with the children?" "Yeah Paula, she will come over, Eddy get your shoes on and go get Paula, tell her it's urgent". "What me"? I asked, "Yes you, I don't see anyone else here called Eddy, for Christ sake, just do as you're told, for once in your life". I stood to do as I was told, then Tim walked towards me and put his hand on my head and ruffled my hair, "Where is Paula? Is she a relative", he asked, "No Paula's my friend, she lives just around the corner on the lane, number 221, and she'll come and watch the kids". Tim then turned to me and said, "You go and sit down, I will get Paula, it's cold and dark outside. I looked up at Tim, he was nice and had a nice gentle smile. I went to sit back on the sofa, Lucy was sitting, still crying, she gave me look. A look that I knew too well, this look meant 'don't come near me, or else'. I was in big trouble, I knew that much, but how could I be blamed for this, I couldn't stop him getting into the car. Not that it mattered to Lucy, she needed someone to blame and that someone was me, again. I should be used to her anger and her hatred towards me by now. I was nine years old, I had always known she didn't like me, just like he didn't like me either and I was now used to this. No matter what I did, it was never right, I got in the way, I was too smelly, or untrustworthy. I was compared to Lucy all the time by him, I could never live up to his expectations. I would never be as pretty as Lucy, as tall as Lucy, as clever as Lucy. He used to say, "Lucy Loo, I love you, you are the apple of my eye". I used to long for a day when he would say he loved me, but it never came, just like my wishes and dreams of the day I would be seen as a pretty girl, a tall girl, who he would show pride in and share some of his love for me. I once wrote a story for English homework during spring bank break. I wrote about what we had done in the holidays, about how happy we were, how we had been to the seaside and had ice cream and rode on the donkeys, and laughed and giggled with excitement about going to the funfair and how she would sit me on her knee and sing to me and how we would all sit and listen to him tell us stories before bed and how they would then kiss us all one by one, good night, sleep tight and god bless. This was just a story for school, this could not be further from the truth of my life. I may not be pretty or tall but I had an imagination that took me away from my life to happier places and I would spend many hours dreaming about how I wished life would be.

Chapter Two

Paula came walking in with hot cocoa for Lucy and I, she then went back to get her cocoa. I liked Paula, she was a small lady, with deep dark brown eyes, a wispy, quiet voice. Paula called everyone "Love", Eddy Love, or Lucy Love, she was a kind lady and had two young daughters who she doted on. She sat on the sofa and reached out her arms to both Lucy and I to come sit either side of her. I moved to sit next to her but Lucy just stood up and went to look out of the window, parting the curtain in the middle, leaning her elbows on the window ledge with her back to the room. Not speaking, but breathing very deeply, she was still angry. "Come on Lucy Love come sit here with me and your sister, it will all be ok, you'll see, you're not doing yourself any good fretting my love, come on, sit with us". Lucy turned around to face Paula, with anger and malice in her face, "No, I'm not going anywhere near her, it's all her fault, if it wasn't for her he would not have got into that car. If he is dead it's her fault, and I won't ever let her forget it". "Now, now, Love, come, come, it's no-one's fault, it's an accident, if it is him at all, your mum said it might not be him" said Paula trying to calm her down. "You really believe that, don't you? Then you're as stupid as her," she said nodding towards me. "That idiot, sat next to you, the one who can't just do one simple thing and stop him getting into the car when he has had a belly full of beer. It's him alright, I just know it, he's had an accident and she's gone to identify the body". Lucy started to cry again, sobbing with her nose running and the tears rolling down her face, she was catching her breath saying, "you can't do one thing right, it's all your fault, it should be you that's dead, not him, oh what's going to happen to us now?" She continued to cry uncontrollably and Paula patted my leg then stood and went to stand beside Lucy. She put her arms round her and then Lucy turned into her as Paula held Lucy and let her cry into her shoulder. Lucy's tears were staining Paula's T-shirt, Paula rubbed her back and just slightly rocked from side to side, she then let out gentle shhhhhhh whilst comforting Lucy.

"Hey what's all this, don't you start as well, or we will all be drowning in tears, mark my words, he will be fine, he's like a cat, he has nine lives that man, believe you me, I know, some of the scraps he's been in, in his time, and every time he comes up smelling of roses".

While I sat watching Lucy get upset and Paula comfort her I had begun to cry, I am not sure why I was crying, was it for myself or for him? I'm still not sure, but I was hurting from deep down inside and I could not stop myself from crying. Was it guilt? Was it all my fault, could I have prevented this from happening? Why had I not run away and then he wouldn't have got into the car? Was there anything else I could do? I didn't know why he got into the car, I wasn't the one driving the other car, I didn't make him crash. Or was I in shock? Whatever it was, I was unable to stop the tears. Paula, still cuddling Lucy, walked with her back to the sofa, bringing Lucy with her to sit next to her on her right side and came to sit by me and cuddled me next to her left side.

I woke up feeling my neck aching, I wasn't sure where I was for a few seconds, then it all came flooding back. "Well hello Eddy Love, you feeling a little better now?" said Paula, in a very hushed and quieter voice, as she then put her index finger to her lip to make sure I was quiet and looked towards Lucy who was sleeping on the other side of her. I looked up and smiled at Paula, I rubbed my neck and then whispered, "What time is it? Have you heard anything yet? Is she not back yet? What do you think is happening?" "Now, now my Love, we have to be patient, I'm sure they will let us know as soon as they can, you know what they say, no news is good news". Paula then winked at me and I smiled back, hoping she was right.

I don't know how long we had all been sat in complete silence, but it felt right to just sit very still and very quiet. I had a bad feeling inside me, a stomach churning feeling, my head was spinning with the memories of the very recent past and what had happened since going to bed last night. This was not going to be a good day today; I just knew it. I found myself thinking about what I would say to my friends at school, when they heard my dad had died? Would I have to stay off school? I didn't like staying off school, I enjoyed school. Lucy would call me a freak, when I would say I didn't want to stay off school, she would do anything to take time off, even pretend she was ill and they would always believe her. Once school had started she would make a miraculous recovery and then they would get to go out for lunch or go shopping and would always have treats when she stayed off school. Not me, I would end up helping with the housework or making cups of tea for the aunties who would call round for a natter and smoke cigarettes whilst discussing what all the neighbours were up to. Who was going on holiday, who was pregnant and who was dodging the loan shark, big Mr Broadbent. I didn't really understand who or what big Mr Broadbent was until I got a lot older and realised this was the name used for the man who all the mums would lend off to pay for Christmas or other luxuries that the wages brought home by the men did not cover. All the children knew about old Mr Broadbent but we were all sworn to secrecy, if any of the dads found out, "all hell would break loose", said mum. She would sit talking with the aunties about how much she had managed to get and what she planned to buy and how long it would take to pay this off before she could have more money from him. I would be sent to sort the bedroom to clean up and then tidy the kitchen and wash the pots and peel the potatoes for tea, whilst they sat chatting as they didn't want me to hear them. Peeling the potatoes was one of my jobs, from as young as I can remember. I did this everyday along with sweeping down the stairs and washing the dishes or drying the dishes and putting them away after tea.

Paula and I then heard a noise from upstairs, it must be one of the little ones, waking up. It was just starting to get light outside, the lightness peaking in through the half opened curtains, the birds were starting to sing. All appeared very normal, like any other day, except it wasn't any other day. I went into the kitchen to put on the kettle as Paula had whispered, go make your auntie Paula a cup of tea Eddy love. I was stood staring out of the kitchen window waiting for the kettle to boil. The small curtains at the kitchen window were never closed, day or night. I could see the dawn breaking. I began daydreaming and thinking about what the day ahead might bring. Would she come home and tell us he was dead? Would she come home and tell us, it's not him? Would he turn up in the car as angry as before? What would we tell him about Paula being here and where had she gone and why had the police been here? Was he somewhere watching the house? Watching us? Not wanting to come back because he knew the police had been here? Did he think the police had come for him and taken her to the station to make a statement about him and what he had done to us last night? I felt my fingers gripping onto the spoon I was holding.

I have no idea what will happen today, will I be able to go to school? Or stay home and do the cleaning? Will he come back before her or will she come back first? What if he was actually dead? Would we have to go to a funeral? What would grandma say? I was cold again, shivering and scared of what will come of us. What would this day bring? Would they make friends again and pretend nothing ever happened like so many times before? I had a feeling things would never be the same after the night's drama.

I spent a lot of the morning thinking about what I

would wear if he had died? What would the funeral be like? Who would go to the funeral? I thought I would wear my school skirt, it's black and people always wear black to funerals on the telly, I assured myself. I don't know what top I would wear; I couldn't remember if I had a black top. Would I be able to get a new one? Would she take us all shopping for new clothes to wear at his funeral? She wouldn't want us to go showing her up. Would we be allowed to go to the funeral, do you have to be an adult? I wasn't sure of any of my questions and the longer I stared out of the window, the more questions came into my mind. I was brought back to the task I had been set by the whistling of the kettle. I continued to make the cup of tea for Paula whilst listening to the boys waking up and moving around upstairs.

Chapter Three

She used to sit on his lap and they would play toy fighting or he would play with my brothers. He would play 'kecky pants'. They all loved this game, I must have been 'soft' or 'a mard arse', like they said, as I didn't like the game, it hurt me. He would grab us and then nip our thighs between his fingers and thumbs, a very quick nip or pinch. It felt like a very quick bite to your skin and left a stinging feeling. I had on the odd occasion that I had joined in been left with tiny little bruises on the top of my legs. I could feel the nip for ages after. The others never seemed to feel the sting of the nip, they just giggled and cried with laughter, jumping around him whilst he would grab each one of them as they ran around him as he sat on the floor with his back resting on the sofa. They would all fall about around him, trying to jump and get away from the nip he would administer whist saying "Kecky pants is coming to get you", in a high pitched voice.

I joined in once, as he was in a good mood. He had come home from work Saturday afternoon. The rain was pouring down outside and we were all sitting watching TV. We sat waiting for the wrestling to start. I would be told to shout for the wrestler opposed to Big Daddy, or Giant Haystacks. My big sister and brothers would sit on the sofa with him in the middle and I would lay on my tummy on the floor, knees bent and my feet in the air. Leaning my chin on my hands. Not the comfiest position, after a while I would get pins and needles in my forearms and hands but I preferred to be on the floor. I could spread out and not be blamed for hitting anyone or leaning on anybody, or worse, making them smell. Lucy would always refuse to sit next to me or have me sitting anywhere near her. We shared a bedroom but she had her own drawers and her side of the wardrobe. I was not allowed to sit on her bed, touch her clothes or even look at any of her things. My nicknames in the family were Eddy, the name I had been known for, as long as I could remember, or Whiff. Despite having a perfectly normal Christian name, I have no recollection of this name ever being used as a child by any family member or even neighbours or friends, I was known as Eddy to everyone except my school teachers, or Whiff by family, mainly Lucy and Peter. I even answered to it, if they shouted, "Whiff can you pass the salt?" I did as requested.

I was a nervous child, always fidgeting and unable to sit still. I was taken to the doctors by mum many times as a small child and was sent to the hospital to discuss my problems. But no cure was ever found. I would continue to wet the bed every night that I slept in my bed in the house we grew up in. I know I smelt, I was told to just get up and get dressed in the mornings for school and Lucy would spend ages in the bathroom which meant I had about 5 minutes to have a wash and get dressed before we were to leave for school. In the winter it was too cold to get into the bath and we didn't have enough money on the electric meter for me to run a full bath every morning. I would use the edge of my face towel run it under the tap to get it wet then rub some soap onto it. After wiping my face and drying it, I would wash as much of the urine off my skin around my private parts and legs. I would strip the wet smelly sheets off my bed most mornings and take it down stairs, put it into the washing machine or washing basket. I would try my best to be discreet about this. If Lucy ever saw me, she would make a fuss, "Oh Whiff, do you have to put that in there now? I'm trying to eat my breakfast and it stinks, you're disgusting, I feel sick now. Hurry up will you and don't think you're sitting next to me, I'm not going to school smelling of piss like you". The little ones would find this funny and giggle and shout Eeewwww, Eddy stinks. It was a game to them, but to me it was embarrassment I could do without. No matter how many times this scenario played itself out, I would never be able to take it on the chin and most occasions I would walk away fighting back the tears that were stinging my eye lids. I would repeat over and over in my mind, 'why me?' Mum or dad never scolded her for swearing at me or being cruel, it was as if she hadn't said a word. No reaction from any of them. I had wished for years that my body would just stop letting me down at night. I had stopped drinking, after 6pm to see if this would stop me from wetting my bed whilst sleeping. I had tried going to the toilet once when I went upstairs to change into my nightdress, then again just before I got into bed but nothing seemed to help. Every morning the same saga would repeat like a bad dream. Every day I would wake up and the feeling of dread and disappointment I felt the minute I realised I was wet and smelling would consume me. Days after day, week after week, month after month the same feelings and fears only added to my already anxious personality.

She took me to see a doctor at the hospital one day. A day I will never forget. I got out of bed as always, washed dressed and took my sheets down to the washing machine. I was told I was to be kept at home today. She told me about the appointment. She would tell me to find some decent clothes for the day as she didn't want me making a show of her dressed like a tramp. I looked through my small wardrobe to find something I felt she may feel acceptable. Every item I showed her was found to be unsuitable. She was getting more and more irritated by me, telling me to just find something decent to wear. I wasn't sure why she disagreed with everything I picked out. After what felt like an hour, I was told to just wear my school clothes as everything else looked tatty. She was shouting at me for not taking care of my things, asking why everything I picked out was either faded, worn or dirty looking. I wanted to say, "Because everything I own was either Lucy's or previously belonged to one of the neighbour's children. I cannot recall any time I was ever taken to buy new clothes just for me, with the exception of my school uniform. We were given tokens for school clothes each year during the summer holidays. I loved the day we went shopping with the tokens as this was the day I would get brand new school clothes, shoes and coat. I would feel very proud and excited to wear my new clothes for the first day of school, where I would look like all the other children and not in worn out or old looking clothes.

Lucy and the boys had all gone to school, she eventually agreed I looked presentable. I was then sent upstairs to wash my face and neck again. She shouted for me to bring her black mid-heel shoes down. As I walked into the lounge with her shoes, I looked up and saw how beautiful she was. I was always proud of her; glad she was my mum. I was often told by the aunties that I looked just like her, "you're the spit of your old mam you are Eddy Love", Paula would say. She used to say I have her stubborn streak as well as her looks. She put on the shoes and this completed her outfit, she was ready to leave. Before she was happy to leave she brushed my hair, scraping the brush over my head pulling my hair into a high pony tail on to top of my head. She would always pull my hair very tight, causing me to wince and moan, I'm head sore and this was a horrible for me to endure. As she scrapped my head with the brush, it felt like my skin was being stretched across my face making my eye lids to feel tightened and stretched. Once she had finished my hair, she stood back, looked at me, "You'll have to do," She said. We then put on our coats and left to get the bus to take us to the hospital for my appointment.

She was different when we were alone, and very different when we went out, whether it was to go to appointments or met new people. Travelling on the bus she let me chose where we sat. I chose to sit downstairs on the seat facing the back seat, so I was riding backwards. She sat facing me, smiling at me. A lady from the next street was sat on the other rear facing seat. "Good morning", she said, "Oh hello Stella, how are you? How's your dad? Getting better I hope? She said. "Well the doctor wants him to stay for observations for the next couple of days, but hopefully if he's up and about soon they will let him come home, I'm taking him to mine. He can't cope at home now; he keeps forgetting things" said Stella. "Oh that will be a squeeze for you love, what does your Howard think about that?" "He can think what he wants, I've told him, if he doesn't like it, then he knows where the door is, my dad has done a lot for him, so if he has a problem, tough". Stella winked at me and smiled. "So where are you off to?" she asked me. "We're going to the hospital too. Going to take her to see the doctor for a check-up" she said before I could answer Stella's question. "How's your Jimmy doing love? Betty next to me said he was on the mend". "He's off the critical list now, they're thinking of taking him off the life support by the end of this week, so he's better than he was but far from being recovered" she said. "Oh dear, you're a brave one for sure, I could throttle my Howard most days, but I'm not sure I could cope if anything like that happened. God bless you love, don't forget to take care of you and your little ones, let the doctors and nurses look after him. And you make the most of your time out of school, sweet pea. You staying off all day and being spoilt by your mummy?" Again she answered before I had chance to open my mouth. "Oh no not this one, she is a little book worm, doesn't like staying away from school, she will go back in after her appointment... anyway how's your Sylvia? I've not seen her for a while. She keeping ok?" She changed the subject so she didn't have to answer any more questions. Once off the bus we waved at Stella as we walked to one side of the hospital for our appointment and Stella went the other way to the wards to visit her dad. As soon as we turned the corner and she was sure Stella was out of ear shot, "She's a right nosey old bird is Stella, she's like the local metro newspaper. Anything you tell her goes all round the estate before you've finished your conversation."

We sat in the waiting room, it was a big room filled with chairs and lots of magazines and a small box with toys for younger children. I was just about to stand up from my chair, when she looked at me and then tapped my leg with her palm. "Just sit still and don't start messing about." I wriggled back onto the chair and sat swinging my legs and reading all the posters and information leaflets on the walls all around the waiting room. We sat waiting to be called in to see the doctor, by the nurse. She sat and then and smiled at me, the smile extended from one cheek to the other cheek, a real smile from her eyes. I noticed this smile and can see it now, in my mind's eye, a big smile, making me feel loved and happy, why can't it be like this every day? I asked myself, she was beautiful when she frowned but when she smiled she was stunning and the look melted my heart and made me feel a warm comfortable feeling inside.

We were called into see the nurse first, I was weighed, asked to stand against a wooden tape measure that was attached to the wall and then nurse would shout out my measurements which would be written down by another nurse. They gave me a small pot and sent me into the toilet, I was asked to provide a sample of urine. I sat in the loo, on tips toes trying to balance over the pot, I seemed to be there for ages, my hand was aching and I could not pee. Oh come on, just pee, I thought, she will be angry if I show her up. I had been warned several times before we got into the hospital. "Make sure you keep your mouth shut, do as you're told and don't be mithering me for drinks and toffees, it costs me enough for the bus fare to come here with you then come back again later to see your dad". Then I managed it, I passed a small amount and managed to get it right into the pot. Pleased with myself, I quickly went outside and handed the pot to the nurse with a big smile on my face, I had done as I was told. She must be pleased with me. I looked at her to see if she was smiling at me, she was looking at her watch and then again at the doctor's door. She did not seem to see I had done everything that was asked of me. I went to sit by her side and as I reached the chair, my name was called again by the nurse, "Edwina Crawley". We stood up together and she patted my shoulder to guide me to the doctor's office where the nurse stood at the door to show us in, to see the doctor. He was sat behind a large wooden desk, he was an older man, with grey hair, a beard and small glasses perched on his nose. He sat reading a pile of papers. We were shown to the chairs and the nurse just nodded and then went to stand with her back to the door behind the doctor. We sat very quiet, I was trying to get comfortable on the chair, wriggling to sit back in the chair when she patted my leg and just looked at me with a very stern look on her face. I stopped moving and sat still. After what seemed like an age, the doctor looked up, over his glasses and nodded at her, then looked at me and said, "Well, well, how are you this fine sunny day? Have you been enjoying the sun with your day off school today?" His smile was kind and warming, he had a very calming and deep voice. I just smiled at him "I'm not having the whole day off school, we came straight here this morning and I am going back to school for my dinner and she is going to go and meet auntie Nora in Stalybridge in the café for a coffee, they have a coffee every Tuesday, after getting her family allowance from the post office" I said. She dragged her chair forward and interrupted me, "I don't like her missing any of her education doctor, it's important, to get a good education these days", she said. Nodding his approval, "yes, yes, of course, and what do you want to do when you grow up?" "I want to be a telephonist, my auntie used to be one and she said I have got the gift of the gab, so I would be good at it". He let out a grin and nodded. I felt like I had grown a foot just sitting in this chair. He was interested in what I had to say and he was listening to me. He then looked back at the papers and said, "Well, you have been brought here to see me today, because you are having a little problem, is that right"? I nodded and then felt like I was shrinking in the chair, my face was starting to heat up and I began to worry, hoping I was going to say everything I had been told to say. I had practised it over and over and she had told me again when we got off the bus, walking up the path to the hospital.

"I was going upstairs, I mean, down stairs and I fell over the dog and hurt my leg. It still hurts and I can't run now because it still hurts". Recited as practiced. "I told her it hurts and she took me to the hospital and they looked at it and put a bandage on it for me. It felt better when I had the bandage but now it hurts again".

"The hospital was near the battered wives refuge we stayed at, but it still hurts me". I looked over to her for approval as I had said exactly what I had been told. As I looked over I could see her face turning blood red as she made a noise as if to clear her throat and then cough, "We went to stay away for a few weeks when she fell on the stairs so she had to go to the local hospital. We were then sent for a check-up by the GP as she's still limping. She had an X-ray of her leg, at the time doctor Gamble and they said she hadn't broken it, but I'm not sure they knew what they were doing. They just seemed to be too busy. They just put on a swab with some cream on it and then bandaged her leg and then sent us home. Now that's not exactly good, for any hospital is it doctor? So I knew that by coming here you would know what's best to do for her. She keeps complaining about this leg and as you can see she will limp on it most of the time". This was partly the truth and the only part they needed to know she had told me, "Do you want the doctors to know that you can't behave and that's why you've got a sore leg? If you hadn't been mithering he wouldn't have kicked you, you know he didn't mean it and they don't need to know you're a pain in the arse, we need them to sort it for you then you can stop whinging about it". The last thing I wanted was for the nice doctor to think I was a naughty girl. The day I got the injury he was angry with my brother for messing with money and losing a pound note. If I had waited until he had calmed down before asking if I could have some money to go to dancing class, then I wouldn't have got the blunt end of his anger. The shock hit me before the pain. I felt a numb hot feeling in the top of my leg causing me to drop to the floor, unable to stand again. I didn't cry at first but when I did start to cry, he just got more angry, "Bleeding delayed reaction, get up and move, get out of my sight before I bleeding cripple you", he said. I scrambled to the door of the kitchen on my bottom, the pain and heat in the top of my leg preventing me from being able to stand up. Why did I not realise that he would be angry? Why did I have to ask for money when he was so angry at money going missing? Why was I so stupid? How did I not see what was coming? She was right, I didn't want the nice doctor to think badly of me. She was protecting me from getting a bad reputation with the doctor and nurse, I knew that then. I believed my recital went well, why was she still looking angry at me? Had I given him the impression I was bad girl? The one impression I was trying so hard to avoid.

Doctor Gamble sat back in his chair and looked at her again, over his glasses, as if he was now digesting this latest piece of information. He then leaned forward and started to write something on the papers. She added "It's probably nothing, she's always been a bit of drama queen, but you can't be too careful can you doctor? I would never forgive myself if she ended up with something seriously wrong with her leg just because that hospital didn't know what they were doing". Again he sat back on his chair and carried on looking at her over his glasses, then he looked at me. "Right now Edwina, can you stand and walk towards the wall at the back of the room please?" I stood up and did as he had asked. "Now walk over to the couch for me". Again I was doing as I was told by the doctor, I walked across the room as he had asked and towards the couch he was pointing to. She was glaring at me, a stare that made me feel uneasy. What had I done wrong? How have I managed to make her angry at me? I did as I was told. I then stood looking down at my feet, not wanting to meet her gaze, I was feeling more and more nervous. "STAND UP STRAIGHT" she said in a very loud and sharp voice. Dr Gamble looked over at her and then at me and said, in a quiet calming voice "Don't worry my dear, your mum is just concerned for your posture, you need to stand tall, and look up, you have a pretty little face, you should be happy to show people, so look straight ahead at me". He said with a smile that reached his eyes. I did as he asked and started to relax, despite her being angry with me.

"So do you think it's anything serious doctor?" she asked. He looked down at his papers and studied them for another few minutes. I was still standing in front of the couch with my head held high. The nurse was still stood by the side of the doctor. He said something to her but I didn't catch what he was saying but I heard the nurse, reply "No, it was negative". He then made a note on the papers. The room was warm, with very white walls and a big picture on the wall of a man standing tall with no skin. The picture showed all the insides of the man and when I noticed it was a man, I let out a giggle. The doctor turned round in his chair and smiled at me, I felt my face heat up with embarrassment. I was thinking to myself, what will I say if he asks what I am laughing at? Luckily he didn't. He turned back to face her and leaned back in his chair, took in a deep breath and said, "It would appear, Mrs Crawley, you may have your appointments mixed up, I am a consultant paediatric urologist and you have been invited here today to discuss Edwina's nocturnal enuresis, or bed wetting problem". He sat forward and smiled at me, as I lowered my head the embarrassment and fear seemed to shoot through me like an electric shock. I had just been walking around the room showing off my leg problem and he was not interested in my leg. She had asked our doctor to send me to the hospital because, I was the only one out of all her five children who was still unable to go two nights in a row without wetting the bed and I was 9 years old now. She would tell any member of our family that would listen, that, "Lucy stopped when she was less than two years old and all the boys were dry by the age of two, so why is it, she's still wetting the bed? She must have something wrong with her?" She repeated this to doctor Gamble, I could no longer look at him directly in the face. He began making more notes and asking her questions about my bed wetting, how many nights per week was I wet? Was the bedroom temperature satisfactory? What, if anything had she tried to help me stop wetting the bed? She told him how she had stopped my fluid intake from 6pm, then would wake me up after my first 3 hours sleep to take me to the toilet and encourage me to go to have a wee in the toilet and not in the bed. I hated this, she would come in, wake me up, "Eddy, come on get up, don't wake Lucy, come on, I don't have all night, get up and go to the toilet, I don't want to be washing your bleeding bedding again in the morning". I remember I would stand from my bed, half asleep and then walk in a daze across the landing to the bathroom. Sit on the toilet and start to fall asleep whilst sitting there and she would shout, "Come on now, you finished yet? I want to go to bed too". I would quickly get myself off the toilet and back to my bedroom and get back into bed. On more occasions than I care to recall, I was woken when she was going to bed and she found I had already wet the bed. She would shout and I would get a slap around my head, "what's wrong with you? You have pissed the bed again, your dirty little bleeder, you stink. Get up, get the bed changed and get your clothes changed." She would walk out of our bedroom and into her room. I would hear him asking what was happening and then he would say, "I'm telling you, she's not normal, she bleeding stinks and makes this house stink too, you need to get her seen to". I would quickly go to the airing cupboard in the middle of the landing and then need to jump to reach the shelf with the sheets. Jumping made a noise on the floorboards and she would dash out of her room towards me, "for god's sake, do you have to wake the whole bleeding house? Get the bedding and get it sorted and get into bed, will you?" I did as I was told and carried the bedding back into my room to change my bed. Lucy turned over in her bed, "Hurry up with the light, Pissy arse". I wanted to shout, "MUUUM, Lucy's swearing at me" but I didn't dare and she knew it. Mum would only agree with Lucy that if I hadn't wet the bed then I would not be having to change it so often. Once I had changed the bed and my night dress I turned off the light and then walked in the dark back to my bed, stubbing my little toe on the leg of the bed, nearly every night. I hopped on my other foot and started to cry, that really hurt, I could not keep it in. Lucy then shouted, "DAAAD, will you tell her, I want to go to sleep, now she's whinging again, I hate this house, why do I have to share a room with her, she stinks". His voice was deep and stern and sent shivers of fear down my spine, "For god's sake, Eddy, get in that bleeding bed and shut it, or I will come in and give you something to cry for." I didn't respond, I hobbled to the top of my bed and got in pulling the covers over my face so Lucy could not hear me crying. My toe felt like I had been hit with a hammer it felt like it had swollen to the size of my thigh, it was throbbing. Some nights when she came in to get me out of bed and I had already wet the bed, she would tell me to just get back into bed. "You pissed in it, you can sleep in it". She would slap me around my head which would make me cry and then shout at me to be quiet and not wake the rest of the house up. I would just get back into bed and try to lay to the side of the wet and cold area of my bed. She didn't tell Dr Gamble about this though. I often spent time in bed wishing I could be the same as everyone else. Thinking why I was the one who couldn't stop wetting the bed? I never found the answer.

I was now stood embarrassed in front of the nice doctor and nurse, I would give anything for him to find out what was wrong with me and show me how to stop wetting the bed or get me the pills that would make me better. Dr Gamble spent some time talking to her about me and every now and again he would look at me and smile or look over to see if I agreed with her, I would just nod my head in agreement. "You do seem to have tried a lot of different tactics, but nothing seems to have made any difference you say? Have you spoken to school to find out how school is going?" I quickly looked at the doctor and then at her, she had been warning me for many years now, that she was going to come to school and tell the teachers and all my friends I was a baby and still wetting the bed. Was he asking if she had done this? Or was he going to tell her to do this? "Well, no doctor, other than family and our own doctor, and now you, I have never discussed this with anyone. You see its embarrassing doctor, I can't tell people I have a nine year-old child who is still not dry at night, it's just not right. Her father thinks she has something seriously wrong with her, I don't mind telling you, I can't keep up with all the washing I have to do, and it's costing me a small fortune every week. She's making my house smell and she has been through several mattresses because she can't hold her own water, it's not good you know, mattresses are not cheap you know doctor". The doctor was nodding and making notes while she was talking. He looked at me and stood up, walking over to me he told me to use the small step and sit on the edge of the couch. I was getting more and more anxious. What was he going to do? He put his hands on either side of my head, and told me to open my mouth and stick out my tongue. Then he asked me to look up and then look down with my chin on my

44

chest. I was doing as he was asking me and I could still see her staring at me from the corner of her eye. The doctor then asked me to swing my legs round onto the bed and relax my head back. He then asked, "Can I just touch your tummy?" I nodded, "Can you lift you blouse up a little for me, then I can touch your tummy?" I did as I was asked, conscious not to lift up too high. "Sorry my hands are a little cold", he said, I jumped a little when his hands touched my stomach, he pressed from side to side, then pressed on my waist and then held my waist from the back on the right side and as he pressed he said "Any pain?", I lay very still just shaking my head, he did the same on the left side and again I shook my head to let him know this did not hurt me. He then used his stethoscope to press on my tummy and put the other end in his ears. He then asked if I wanted to listen, I nodded eagerly. Dr Gamble then held the stethoscope on my tummy and let me listen to the growling sounds it was making. "Can you hear that?" he asked. Again I smiled and nodded to him, "that's your breakfast moving around and feeding you to keep you healthy". He then removed the stethoscope and asked me to sit up and he listened to my back. I'm not sure what he was expecting to hear, I wasn't aware my back would make any sounds. He then told me to pull my blouse back down and come and sit with her at his desk. He did some more writing as we just sat in silence. The nurse was still standing behind him. She looked fed up, not smiling or making any eye contact with any of us. I started to wonder why she was just standing in the room doing nothing and saying nothing. I don't much fancy being a nurse if they just stand behind the doctors. I thought nurses made people better and gave out tablets, not just stand to attention like a soldier behind a doctor.

Dr Gamble then put his pen down and looked up over his glasses at me, "Well my dear, we have some good news and some not so good news. The good news is you're a very healthy young lady, a little on the small side but you have a small frame so it's to be expected. The bad news is; we have no medicine or magic potion that will help you with your problem. Your mum appears to have tried lots of different methods to try to help you with this problem but it still persists". I nodded and so did she, then she let out a sigh, "So what am I supposed to do with her doctor? Just let her keep wetting the bed? Causing my whole house to smell and spend hours washing the bed clothes? Will she grow out of it? Why is it she is the only one in my family that is still doing this?" Doctor Gamble sat very calmly listening to her. "Well like I said you have tried a lot of different tactics, and I take my hat off to you for doing this. You seem to have tried as much as you can to help your daughter without making her feel embarrassed or ashamed but you have not yet been successful with any of them." She looked over at me smiling "It's not her fault doctor, I believe it's an illness, no child would do this on purpose, so her father and I feel we should just help her through this problem and not make her feel ashamed or embarrassed. Her brothers and sister are aware it is not her fault and have on occasion tried to poke fun at her for this, but my husband and I stop this immediately which helps them understand this is a problem not to be

laughed at. Together we are a very accepting family, doctor"
She said all this whilst looking at me with a smile on her face
and a look of pity. "Well she is a very lucky young lady to
have such understanding parents. I hope you realise this
Edwina?" Doctor Gamble then looked at me for my response.
I smiled and nodded. "She goes shy whenever we have to
talk about it doctor", she said. "No matter," said Doctor
Gamble. "You have just given me an idea. We have just
received a device for trial and this has only been given to
families who are supportive of the child's problems. I was
thinking we could try this new device? If you're willing to give
it a trial?" he looked down at me when he asked this? She
looked at me with a smile and replied for me, "Yes of course
she wants to try it, don't you Edwina? You would try anything
if it means you can go and stay over with friends more and
not worry about embarrassing yourself, don't you?" I
nodded, not sure what this device she was agreeing to, was
going to mean for me. Doctor Gamble must have sensed my
fear and said, "Don't worry little lady, it's not anything that
will hurt you, it's discreet and you can keep it in your
bedroom and only you and your family will know about it. It's
called a bedwetting alarm, you will have a mat under your
sheet and any moisture that it detects will set off an alarm in
a little box that you keep next to your bed, to wake you up,
so you can go and use the bathroom as you are disturbed
from sleep when your bladder decides to empty. Your body
will hopefully get used to this system and start to wake you
before your bladder releases the urine." It sounds good from
what he was saying but something inside me was still unsure.

I felt I needed to wait until I actually saw the alarm itself. "Well if you are happy to give this a try I can arrange for this to be ordered and delivered to this unit and you will be sent a letter to come and collect the alarm and one of the nurses will show you how to use it safely", said Dr Gamble. She smiled at me and said, "She will be so much happier with this alarm to stop her from wetting the bed, won't you Eddy?" She said. "Can I just clarify this is not a curing device this device can only help to try train the brain to wake her from sleep when the bladder decides it needs to empty, there are no guarantees this will work but is worth trying as you have trialled so many different techniques, with little success". She appeared to deflate a little after this information, then said, "I know you have to say this, but I'm sure you wouldn't offer this if you didn't think it would help her, thank you doctor, we are very grateful, aren't we Edwina?". I nodded my agreement as expected. "Don't look so worried my dear, if this does not work you will grow out of it, I have had many children come to see me for this over the years and all of them stopped wetting the bed before adulthood. So be sure this will stop one day."

One thing we didn't share with the doctor was, I managed to stay dry when staying over at my aunt and uncle's house and that I had never had an accident anywhere else, even on the odd occasion I had stayed over at friends. I was always concerned before going to bed when staying out, that I might embarrass myself and would make sure I went to the bathroom before settling to sleep, but I had never needed worry as I had never wet any other bed but my own bed at home. Even I knew this was odd at nine years old but she wouldn't let me tell the doctors this. "Don't be stupid, you tell any doctor that and they will just say it's something at home that is causing this and that's ridiculous. Keep your trap shut and let me do the talking", was what she had said a few weeks ago when we went to see the GP about this as she said she had, had enough of all the washing and having her house smell of piss all the time because of her bone idle kid who would rather piss the bed than get up and use the toilet like normal folks.

Chapter Four

Mum was standing in the lounge with her large mirror, taken off the wall and propped up at the side of the TV which was sat in the corner on top of the coloured stone fireplace. She was applying her makeup, she used Lecher foundation first and I would stand below her watching how she applied her makeup. She would cover her face to remove all her freckles and blemishes. Not that she had many blemishes, she was very pretty. She would put on pink rouge to her cheeks with a large thick flat lipstick and she would pout and suck in her cheeks then rub the rouge into her cheek bones. Then she used a black pencil to colour her eyelids and eyebrows in and then she would stand leaning into the mirror with her mouth and eyes open wide, stretching her face to apply her mascara to the top eye lashes. She was an expert at this, she did it every morning after she had blown her hair, back combed it and applied hair lacquer to keep her hairstyle in place, guarding her eyes with her other hand and I would stand back to avoid the toxins from the spray. She had short hair and would have a colour put on it at the hairdressers every once in a while or she would ask Paula to put a packet colour on for her whilst sitting in the kitchen. Paula came to our house at least once per week for a chat and coffee or tea. Paula had two sugars in her coffee and no sugar in her tea. I knew exactly how all the aunties preferred tea or coffee, sugar or milk, as I was told often, "Eddy go make a brew", every time someone came round to our house. A lot of the time, she would go out to visit her friends. She would 'just nip to see Auntie Paula or Auntie Nora or round to her friend on the next street, called auntie Brenda'. She would spend a lot of time at her friends' homes. We would be left at home, she would tell Lucy she was in charge and then leave her instructions before going out. "Eddy wash the pots and make sure you peel the potatoes for tea and chip them. Do enough for all of us. Lucy keep your eye on the little ones and dry the pots and boys, tidy your bedroom before I get home, and all of you, behave, do you hear me?" Off she would go then to her friends. I hated it when she went to visit her friends, she would be gone for ages and Lucy would start to make fun of me, or start to boss me about, she would end up threatening to hit me if I didn't wash and dry the pots. If I still refused this she would often hurt me, pulling my hair or just slap me across the face. My reactions were always slower than her. I never knew it was coming, no matter how many times she did it and she always caught me with a hard slap or grab my hair and pulled me to the floor until I cried my submission and ended up agreeing to do all the jobs. She would tell me to do as I was told or she would go to school and tell all my friends I wet the bed and that my nickname was Whiff because I was a pissy arse and no one in our house even liked me. She would say all this in front of the little ones who would join in with her. "Pissy arse, Pissy arse, Eddy is a Pissy arse". The slaps stung for a few minutes but the name calling really hurt me deep inside. I was left feeling I hated my life and my siblings. I would be washing the dishes and drying them whilst crying, saying "I'm going to tell mum when she gets back. You always leave me to do everything". I would try to keep the tears at bay and not let her see how upset I was but I never managed this, she knew how to hurt me and she knew that by getting the little ones to join in I would feel even worse. They all seemed to enjoy the spectacle, as they were a group and I was the one to ridicule while they were spending nice time, either colouring in, drawing or watching the children's programs on TV. I could hear the laughter from the kitchen, they were watching TV and all laughing at the same time, they all seemed to be good friends. I was never part of this laughter, I don't know why, I must have irritated all of them all. I would spend my time alone daydreaming about my future and my children. I won't let my children pick on each other, they will love each other and be best friends, they would not leave anyone out of the fun and laughter, I wouldn't spend all my time at my friends' houses, I would spend my time with my children all having fun and colouring or watching TV together. By the time I had finished daydreaming I had washed and dried the dishes and peeled and chipped a pan of potatoes, I was quite good at peeling potatoes, I did this nearly every evening of my childhood as this was one of my jobs, I was able to do this at speed by the time I was nine years old. She would always come back from visiting her friends after everything was done. I used to wish she would turn up and see Lucy sitting doing nothing with the little ones and me having to do everything, but no that never happened. I would try to get to her to tell her what had happened before Lucy spoke to her. She would walk into the lounge, see them all sat watching TV and as I started to tell her about Lucy hitting me and making me do her jobs, but she would just roll her eyes at me, "Oh for god's sake Eddy, stop with your bloody whinging. Why is it every single time I nip out, you are being picked on? Change the bloody record, will ya. Have you done the potatoes?" This was how it played out every time. I never stopped trying to tell her of how unfair I felt my life was, how my siblings would gang up on me and bully me to do all the jobs or use my bed wetting problem against me as a threat.

Whilst watching her put on her makeup I looked up to her and asked, "You going to the hospital again today?" She stopped applying her lipstick and looked down at me. She stared at me for a while before replying, "Yeah, where else do you think I'm going? To visit the queen?" I noticed something in her tone when she spoke, she didn't seem to be very happy about her visit today. I couldn't put my finger on what the problem may be but I knew she was anxious. She sipped her tea and then leaned forward, looked in the cup and screwed up her nose, "Urrghhh, that's gone cold, make me another brew Eddy". I did as I was told and went into the kitchen to make her a brew. I couldn't stop thinking about her reaction when I asked about her going to the hospital. She had been going to visit him daily, for what felt like months. I'm not sure exactly how long he had been in hospital but I did know he was very lucky to be alive and that he was now out of danger. They had moved him a few days ago. Where they had moved him to, I'm not sure. I'd overheard her telling auntie Paula that they said he is out of danger and can have other visitors now and this was a couple of days ago. Lucy had been to see him last night, she had been allowed to stay up late and took a card she had made for him and some sweets. She had come home late, I was in bed and sleeping, when she came into our bedroom, banged the door against the bottom of my bed and switched on the light. I did wake up but I didn't open my eyes, I heard mum's voice from the landing, "Oh for god sake, Lucy keep the noise down you don't want to wake pissy arse up". I felt the hurt building inside me, 'why would she say that? Why am I such a problem? I just don't understand my family'. I drifted back off to sleep with a heavy feeling in my chest.

I took her a fresh brew and put this on the fireplace at the side of the mirror and her makeup. I could just about reach the top of the fireplace with the cup. We had a coloured stone fireplace, it was built by one of his friends a few years ago. Everyone used to comment on it when they came to our house, it had pink, yellow, grey and stone coloured bricks. It had boxes lined with dark wood and she put ornaments in the boxes. As the TV was on the top of the fireplace, you could sit on the chair or sofa and watch TV and the little ones could play nearby or in front of the TV, but would not block the TV as this fireplace stood quite tall. I wondered if I should ask her about him. Was he well enough to come home? Would he be going back to work when he gets out of hospital? He was a long distance lorry driver so he would spend quite a lot of time away from home working. Therefore, him being in hospital did not have much of an impact on our life as we were used to him being away for long periods of time. The difference was, instead of going to visit friends she would be going to visit him in hospital. She was now standing back admiring her make-up and outfit. She was wearing a navy pencil skirt, white blouse and navy cardigan with American tan tights and black pointed stilettos. She turned to the side and looked at herself in the mirror and then looked back over her shoulder to check her outfit at the back, then turned to the other side and did the same again. She was now done and ready to leave. She looked down at me and said, "Will I do?" not that my opinion mattered to her but she liked to be complimented. I nodded my head and smiled up at her, she looked beautiful, I thought. "Make sure this house is tidy when I get home and no messing about, I won't be long, should be back for tea. Paula's at home so if you need anything nip round, but don't be mithering her, do you hear me?" I nodded again, the smile on my face was now gone. The lounge was a tip, all her make-up, hairspray, hair brushes and heated rollers and hairdryer were left on the fireplace with her cold cup of tea I had made her earlier and her ashtray full of cigarette ends. Some of her clothes were left on the chair, where she had thrown them as she had been trying on different pieces before deciding on the outfit she was now wearing. The kitchen was a tip, a sink full of dirty pots, the sides full with open cereal boxes, milk bottles and used tea bags and cups. I set about clearing her makeup and carrying this upstairs to put it away in her bedroom. I was the only one at home as the others were all at school. She had kept me off school to help her sort out the house. I hated staying off school as I would have to spend the day cleaning and missing my friends at school. I once moaned at being kept off school, "aww do I have to? We've nearly finished reading our book in story time and I really want to know how the book ends", I said. "You want to know how a bloody book ends. You need to learn how to get on in life not in bleeding books young lady, not read stories and fill your head full of magic. You need to know how to keep yourself and your home clean. Let me tell you. You won't find a husband who wants to live in a fairy tale. I really don't know how I ended up with you. You should spend more time with your head in the real world lady and out of them stupid books", she said. I never moaned out loud about being kept off school again.

She never kept Lucy off or the boys, only me, "I need you to help me out today, I can't do everything myself and go to the hospital to visit him. It won't do you any harm to have one day off". Except it wasn't just one day off, it was at least one day off per week. I hated being kept off school, I enjoyed school, spending time with my friends and having fun, being a child and not an adult. I enjoyed learning, enjoyed the interaction and the games we would play at lunch time, pretending we were characters out of our favourite programs and playing them out in the playground whilst avoiding the boy's football as they played in the centre of the playground and we played on the outskirts. I enjoyed listening to the stories about what my friends were doing on the weekends, and what games they would play at the end of the day when they would all be meeting up to play out on their own streets. I would tell them about the things I had been doing with my family and how much fun I had with my brothers and sister and how we would all spend time chatting and laughing together. I would paint a picture of a very different home than the one we actually lived in. I would avoid Lucy in the playground, I would not want my friends to see how she responded to me when she saw me. I managed to keep the whole story going for most of my childhood years, letting all my friends know how happy we were as a family and how we all took care of each other and how my big sister would protect me if she thought I was in any danger. I didn't believe this for a second but I wished I could believe it. I so wanted to be part of a loving and happy family. I hated being the butt of all the jokes and hated myself for being weak and not being able to stand up for myself against my siblings. I hated the fact I was the one that wet the bed, the one he could not abide and the one who she chose as her cleaner.

It was Saturday afternoon and she was taking Lucy with her to visit him. I overheard her telling Nora earlier "he's been moved to a ward now and the kids can go see him, I can't take the boys, I don't think he is ready for them yet, but he has been asking to see Lucy, I don't think Eddy wants to go yet, you know how she is, it'll probably upset her too much. Lucy hasn't stop asking to see him since the night of the accident so I have to take her". At the weekend, hospital visiting was more relaxed and visitors were allowed to go and see relatives for the most part of the day but only two per bed, she said. Nora had taken the boys with her earlier and they had all been warned to behave or they will be in big trouble and won't get toffees that she had promised when she comes home. I was allowed to stay home alone. "You stay here and tidy up for me, that'll be a great help". I wanted to complain and ask why I couldn't go with Nora and play or sit and watch TV at her house, but I knew that would be pointless, she needed me to stay and clean the house and get the potatoes peeled for tea. I liked being alone on my own in the house, I could spend the time thinking and day dreaming. It would take me some time to clean up today. She stood at the lounge room door and shouted for Lucy to come down stairs, it was time for them to walk around the corner and get the bus to the hospital. Lucy came running down stairs, all smiles and excitement. She had not stopped talking about how she was going to tell him about her new shoes and she was going to ask if she can have her spending money put up so she can go to the Friday disco at the local town hall. All her friends had started to go but Lucy had been told she has to wait and see what he says. "If I let you go and he finds out, he will kill me, you can wait until he is well enough for you to visit and you can ask him yourself", she said. "Oh I will, I know he'll let me, as long as I tell him our Peter is going and he is going to walk me to the disco and back home, he will be fine". Peter is our cousin, he is 16 and in the final year at school, he is a good boy and always liked to spend time with Lucy and her friends. One of the popular boys from school, Steve Connor, likes Lucy and when Peter is with her he gets to hang around with Steve and his group of friends. Steve Connor smokes and so does Lucy when she is out with them. I have seen her smoking at school. I threatened to tell on her but she then threatened to tell everyone in school that I still wet the bed. So of course I never told on her and she knew I wouldn't.

I had cleaned all the house and peeled enough potatoes for tea and had just sat down on the sofa when Nora arrived with the boys, they came in with mud all over their shoes. "Take your shoes off", I shouted. Nora put her hands to her ears and said, "Eddy, stop shouting, its only mud, it will hoover when it's dry". I was still stood staring at the mess they were making. Peter was in the fridge getting the milk out, Luke was running upstairs with his muddy shoes on and Jimmy was pulling the stool up in front of the fireplace to put on the TV. Nora sat on the lounge chair nearest the door, "your mum and Lucy should be back soon, make me a brew Eddy. I'll stay with you until they get here". She made herself comfortable and kicked off her slippers. Off I went to the kitchen to make her a brew.

They came rushing into the house, both wet through from the rain, Lucy had a kagool on, (a very thin waterproof mac you could fold up into a small bag and take this with you anywhere as it was lightweight), but this was stuck to her clothes and her fringe was peeping through the hood, rain dripping from them both. They stepped into the hallway with the door now shut behind them and shook themselves, Lucy trying to take off her kagool with difficulty as it had now started to stick to her body. She eventually pulled it over her head and kicked off her white pumps, they were now a dirty blue/white colour. The blue colour from her jeans had run onto her pumps as they got wet from the rain. She ran upstairs to get changed. Mum went into the lounge after kicking off her shoes and taking off her coat and throwing this onto the stairs whilst she stood behind the closed front door. I had been sitting in the lounge when they arrived and I went and stood with Nora at the lounge room door. "Eddy go and get your mum a towel to dry herself, then make her a brew, will ya?" said Nora. I did as I was asked, running upstairs to the airing cupboard to get the towel. Then quickly ran down the stairs and tripped on one of the boy's shoes that had been kicked off and landed on the 4th stair. Landing heavily on my face at the bottom of the stairs, hurting my chin as it scrapped against the carpet. I hit my left elbow and landed with my right wrist stretched out in front of me, as I tried to stop myself from any further injury. I grazed both knees and shins on the carpet and began to cry. Mum came out of the lounge almost immediately, she stood over me, shouting "Oh for Christ sake Eddy, get up, stop being bleeding stupid and go make me a brew, your whinging is the last thing I need after the day I have just had". She pulled the towel from underneath me which caused my right wrist to twist against it, sending more pain shooting into my hand and up towards my elbow as I was still holding it with my fist clenched. I screamed out in pain, "Oh Jesus, anyone would think you had been in a major accident, you wanna go up there and look at the state of him, let me tell you, you wouldn't be such a bleeding drama queen. He's lucky to be alive and you're screaming about a little fall. Now get up, make me a brew or I will give you something to cry about".

As I tried to lean on my hands to get up, the pain in my right wrist sent an electric shock through my hand. I winced in pain as I tried to hold back the tears from running down my face. As I walked into the kitchen, she walked back into the lounge. I looked down at my legs, my shins and knees, were grazed and stinging, from scraping the carpet. I couldn't touch the sore bits. I lifted the kettle using my left hand and filled it up with water, trying to use the painful right hand to turn the tap. The pain increasing as I tried to put pressure on the taps. Still crying with pain and stinging but keeping as quiet as I could, so she couldn't hear me. I eventually made her a cup of tea and managed to carry this into the lounge to her, using my left hand. I was limping in and holding my right arm across my tummy due to the pain. "Oh for god sake, walk properly, I won't tell you again, you tripped, you didn't fall off a cliff". I cried even more at this and was really struggling to keep my tears in. I turned to walk out of the lounge, trying not to limp. "Eddy, pass me the ashtray off the window ledge". She said. Turning round to pass her the ashtray I walked passed Nora who was still sitting on the chair, Nora looked at me and gave me a sympathetic nod and then wink as I limped passed her with the ashtray. "Now sod off, and tell that lot to keep it down". The boys were upstairs, it sounded like one was crying, one was jumping on a bed and I could hear Lucy arguing with Jimmy, he was shouting "I need the toilet". Lucy shouted back to him, "You'll have to wait, STOP banging on the door, I'm warning you". I limped upstairs slowly, the pain in my legs increasing with every step. As I got to the top, Jimmy ran past me, knocking my right hand into the wall. I screamed in pain, I was now sat on the top stairs holding my arm across my body. Jimmy giggling as he ran past. I saw him barge though the lounge door, "Mum Lucy won't let me have a wee, and I'm bursting". Mum came out of the lounge pushing the lounge door so hard it swung back and slammed shut again, she started to run up the stairs I quickly stood to get out of the way. "Right I've had it with you lot, you, shut it". She said to me. "LUCY, get out of that bathroom and let him in, if he pisses his pants, I'll be blaming you. Now get out. Peter, Luke, quit the noise, I've got a bleeding headache with you both, you're all going to bed early tonight, I'm not putting up with this all bleeding night, don't you lot know I've got enough to worry about without coming home to this mad house". Then the noise ceased, the boys went quiet and Lucy walked, stamping her feet across the landing to our shared bedroom.

I walked to my bedroom and sat on my bed nursing my arm. Lucy walked in from the bathroom. She had been washing her hair. "Oh what's up with you? Don't tell me, you've scratched yourself". "Shut it you, I might have broken my arm and no one cares, it's killing me, look it's started swelling up". I looked at my wrist again and then looked down at my legs. I had a bruise and some swelling on my shin, along with a graze on my knees. "Ooooooh, no one cares, I might have broken my arm" Lucy said mocking me. "You better shut it, mard arse. You haven't broken anything, so don't think your sitting their whinging, if you don't shut it, you can get out of here". I sat looking at her, why was she so horrible? I had never done anything to her, she has no reason to be so unkind and nasty. I sat feeling very sad and pained, thinking to myself, "I hate this house, I hate this family, and I wish I was dead. If I've broken my arm, they will all know about it". I wouldn't say I thought they would all be sorry because I do not believe this to be the case, I believe they would not be bothered at all about my health, only that I may not be able to clean up as well or peel potatoes as fast.

Chapter Five

Six weeks school summer holidays, when most kids loved this time of year. Not me, I hated being off school, I missed spending time with my friends and learning new things, reading books. I was looking out of the window, sitting near the back of the bus upstairs on my way home from the swimming baths with Lucy and the boys. She had got her family allowance this morning and said we could all go to the swimming baths so long as we stayed together and Lucy and I looked after the little ones. We often went to the swimming baths together on school holidays or on a Sunday afternoon. Then we didn't need a bath for school on Monday. The boys had got onto the bus before Lucy and I then ran upstairs and sat at the back of the bus. We got on the bus and followed them to the seats and all sat together. I sat gazing out of the window and although I had seen this route many times before I was not paying any attention to the scenery as I started to daydream. 'What will he be like when he gets home? Will he be happy to see us? Will he now be a nicer person after this accident'? She always seemed to be in a good mood when she gets home after visiting him, maybe that was because he was now being nice. She had said he was in a coma for the first two weeks due to a head injury, she told everyone who called, they weren't sure if he was going to make it, he has had four major operations and they said it was touch and go. She would always start to get tearful whenever she told anyone about this. She said, until they woke him up, they weren't sure if he was going to be able to breath on his own. The day they woke him up she came home and said, once he was awake and breathing for himself, the doctors said, he will get stronger and stronger with every day that passes. He has been in hospital for many months, I had gotten used to our new way of life. We never saw him and she was always either round her mates letting them know how he was doing or up at the hospital visiting him. I was anxious about his return home. I kept thinking, everything was going to change again. She wouldn't need to go out so often, as she wouldn't be visiting him in hospital. "Listen you lot", she said one night just before the boys and I were sent up to bed. "Your dad should be coming home soon. So, I'm going to need your help when he gets home, I need you all to be good, do you hear me? No messing about, no fighting or falling out and making sure you all keep your rooms tidy, no mithering him and keeping the noise down, he is going to need lots of rest and help the nurses said". "When is he coming home?" asked Jimmy. "As soon as the doctors and nurses think he is ready to come home. He is doing well every day and they said yesterday that it won't be long before he is up and about and eating solid foods. Are you going to help me take care of him?" she said. Jimmy just looked up at her and then looked down as if he were contemplating his response. "What will I have to do?" he asked. She let out a giggle, "Don't look so worried, it's only your dad, you can fetch his slippers when he needs them, or turn over the TV when he asks. Do you think you could do that?" Jimmy then nodded his acceptance of the new tasks then continued to walk upstairs to bed. 'Eating solids? I thought. What has been eating all this time? Will he be thin? My mind was full of questions, but I never found the right time to ask about them. The bus stopped and Debbie got on with her mum. Debbie was one of my friends from school, one of the girls I had told all my fantastic family stories to. I was with my brothers and sister, just like I had told them, we were happy spending time together, having adventures, playing games and having fun in everything we did. I looked up and said, hiya, to Debbie. She smiled and said hiya back. "Ooooooohh Whiff has a friend, Hiya," Luke said mocking me. Debbie just turned and looked at him and then at me. She then turned back to face the front and sat down next to her mum. Jimmy and Peter all started to laugh at him and then all of them giggling and mocking me, "Ooooooooh, hiya" they said, over and over. I looked at them and tried to show my angry face to see if this would stop them. "Shhhhhhh", I said. They continued mocking me, "Ssssssssssssssssshhhhhhhhhhh", they said now in a chorus. The bus was now reaching our stop, we all stood up and started to walk down the isle of the bus towards the stairs, holding onto each chair as we walked down the bus. Once I got to Debbie, I looked down at her and said, "See ya," She just looked at me and nodded. I wanted to stop and make an excuse for my brother's behaviour but didn't have the time, the bus was nearly at my stop, so I continued to walk towards the stairs. The boys and Lucy all carried on walking down the stairs whilst the bus was moving, I stood at the top of the stairs, I was scared of falling, so waited until the bus came to a stop and then made my way down the stairs as fast as I could before the bus set off again. Peter and Jimmy were now looking up at the top deck of the bus waving to Debbie and her mum. Luke had started to run ahead, "Luke, STOP, right there" shouted Lucy. I pushed Peter in the small of his back to stop him mocking me waving to Debbie. Peter then turned and without warning he punched me in my stomach, winding me. I was trying to cry but the punch had taken my breath away. I stood unable to move from the spot, holding my arms across my stomach. Peter and Jimmy stood for a second and started giggling at me, then ran off to catch up with Lucy and Luke. Tears now streaming down my face, I slowly began to walk behind them. I eventually caught up with them all at the top of our garden path. The boys ran into the house to tell mum about the tricks they had been able to perform in the pool. She stood for a minute listening to them and then told them to go play in the garden until tea time. I was told to go sort out the wet swimming costumes and towels and put them into the wash basket then peel the potatoes for tea. Lucy went to join mum sitting in the lounge watching the TV listening to mum's update on how dad was recovering in hospital.

We had eaten tea and were all ready for bed. I stood staring at the TV, not watching it, I was in a daydream again. "Eddy, I won't tell you again, up to bed and make sure you go to the toilet first, the last thing I need is you pissing the bed again". I jumped as I had gone into a world of my own again thinking about her earlier statement about him being put on solid food soon, wondering what he had been eating. I quickly came back round when she shouted at me and I walked past her scowling. Why did she always have to do that? Peter and Luke were stood at the top of the stairs, shouting, "Pissy arse, Pissy arse" and giggling to themselves. She laughed too, walking past the stairs into the kitchen. "Right stop it now, its bed time, I don't want to hear another peep out of you lot". I was at the top of the stairs scowling at the boys who were still giggling and chanting "Pissy arse, Pissy arse" in a hushed tone, so she couldn't hear them. I walked past them, into the bathroom and slammed the door shut, so they knew they had upset me. With that all three boys, shouted in a chorus, "Whooooooooooo" then started to giggle. I sat on the loo, very close to tears, I hated my life. I was conscious not to let them see they had upset me. If they knew I was upset, they would just continue with the teasing. I stayed in the bathroom for a few more minutes and composed myself before walking out of the bathroom, past the boy's room and to my bedroom. I walked in and closed the door behind me. I could no longer hear the boys teasing me. Why, I thought to myself, was it, I was the butt of all the jokes in this house? They all made fun of me. I never felt like I fitted in. Was Lucy right? Was I adopted? She'd said this many times to me and for many years. It made sense to me, except we all looked alike, everyone would say so. "Oh Eddy love, you're the spitting image of you mum". Paula always said this. He used to say this too except he wouldn't be so nice about it. "You're just like your bloody mother," he would say. "Not only do you look alike, you're a bleeding waste of space too", whenever they had fallen out. Surely I can't be adopted and still look like her. If this wasn't the case, then, they just didn't like me. Simple as that. I could cope with not being liked by them all, but being teased and picked on day in, day out was horrible. Why could I not just ignore them as Paula used to say, "oh they don't mean it Eddy love, it's just families for you, we're all the same, we all poke fun at each other in our house, we don't take it to heart though, you're just a sensitive little lady". But that's just it, WE don't make fun of each other, I always seem to be the topic of ridicule. I never sit with my brothers laughing at Lucy's problems, she doesn't have any, she is perfect, pretty, tall and never does anything wrong. WE don't poke fun at any of the boys, they laugh together at each other but mainly at me. I would sit and ponder these thoughts, I could never recall a time when any of my siblings or my parents were the one being made fun of. Not that I could make fun of them, I knew all too well how hurtful it was, I could not do that to anyone else. Maybe Paula was right, I am just too sensitive, maybe I need to toughen up?

Chapter Six

We only ever had one family holiday, we went to a caravan park in Wales. We had been told about the holiday as a group one Saturday evening before he went to work as a pub bouncer. He would work outside one of the local pubs. He did it every Friday and Saturday night for as long as I could remember. He would get washed and dressed in a black suit and a Dickie bow. He told us his job was to stand on the doors of the pubs and make sure everyone who went into the pub was on their best behaviour and if anyone caused any trouble or started to misbehave, his job was to talk to the people who were not being good and stop any trouble. He was a big man, around six feet tall and large arm muscles, that he would flex to show us. He would sit chatting to the boys at tea time and tell them to eat the vegetables so they too could grow to be big and strong like him and Popeye the sailor who ate nothing but spinach and had huge muscles to save Olive Oil from evil. Every weekend he would be getting ready to go out to work at the pub. I would stand by the sink in the kitchen, watching him shaving his chin. He would use a small brush, wet this and then brush the soap with it to make a lather and then put this soapy lather on his chin that made him look like he had a beard like Santa. Then he would carefully pull faces as he used his razor to shave all the black bristles from his chin, I was fascinated with this. He would then wipe the remaining soap off his chin with a towel and slap his cheeks and say, "Look at that Eddy, smooth as a babies bum". This made me giggle, no matter how many times he said it. He would then get his aftershave, pour some into his hands and then slap his chin and cheeks with it. Like clockwork he would then say, "oh Jesus," as the aftershave would sting his skin. I would instantly stop giggling; I was conscious he was not too happy with the sting. He was known by many around our little town as a gentle giant, or Peter Pan, as he had a reputation for being very calm but able to handle himself and no matter how old he got, he, never seemed to age. He was a handsome man, in my eyes, but not always a nice man. I would always find it difficult to understand how so many people thought he was so nice, when he could be so different when the front door to our house, was closed.

We were all sat in the lounge watching and laughing at the TV. Lucy was sat on the chair beside him and Jimmy was sat with his feet up on the sofa with Luke cuddled up to her at the other end. Peter was sat across the other chair, his head on one arm and his feet resting on the other arm. I was lying on my tummy on the rug in front of the fire, leaning up on my elbows and resting my head on my hands. The adverts came on as he walked into the lounge then Lucy stood up. "Sit down will ya, we've got something to tell you all". "No, I'm going the toilet", said Lucy. "Just sit down and wait a minute can't ya? I said we've something to tell ya all". Lucy huffed and sat on the edge of the chair, impatiently staring back at her. "Hurry up, or I'm going to wee myself". He leaned over and patted Lucy on the shoulders, she then looked up and gave him a forced smile. "Give your mum a minute, I think you'll like this". Lucy just huffed again and folded her arms across her chest. "Don't tell me, you're not going to have another baby are you? I'm not having my spending money cut if you are". The boys all sat up ready to listen, "Oh I hope it's a boy, I don't want another girl, not like pissy arse" said Jimmy, this made them all burst out laughing, mum and dad joined them laughing too. I didn't see why they all found this so funny or why I always had to be the one they made fun of. "I don't want another smelly boy, anyway you won't have enough room in that bedroom to fit another one", that stopped them all from laughing. We all looked to her to hear what she was going to say. "Now, stop it you lot, no more babies for this family" she said. None of us moved as we were eager to hear what she was going to say. I sat up on the rug and crossed my legs, sitting facing her, waiting to hear her news. While the boys were guessing and he was sat calming Lucy down, "no one is going to be taking a cut of spending money, so calm yourself down misses" I began to wonder to myself, was she going back to work again? Were we going to move house? Oh no, had someone died? Wait he said we would like it. It can't be a death. I sat up with my back straight, feeling nervous. "Who wants to go on holiday?" she said. The boys let out a cheer. Yeahhhhhhhhhh me, me, me, they shouted and then started to jump up and down on the chair and sofa like they were jumping on a trampoline, full of excitement and happiness. Lucy jumped up and wrapped her arms around his neck? He leaned in and kissed her on her forehead. "Told you, you would want to hear this". I was smiling from cheek to cheek just as excited as my siblings, as I was on the carpet I could not bounce. I stood up for a minute or so and then sat waiting to find out where we were going. "Hush will you all, then I can tell you where we are going", she was laughing at the boys who were now all running along the sofa, chanting, "we're going on holiday, we're going on holiday. We didn't ask the name of the caravan park, it was a holiday, it could have been in the local park for me. A holiday, was something I heard my friends talking about every year after the six weeks school summer holidays. We had never had a family holiday before, we were so excited, the boys started to jump about and giggle tickling each other and screaming yesssss, yesss. "Does it have a beach? Can we have ice-cream? Can we go swimming every day? Billy went swimming every day when he went to Blackpool" said Peter, these were just some of the questions from the boys.

"We have booked us all a week on a campsite, in a lovely 8-berth caravan for a week in Wales, it's got a pool, kid's club and disco, crazy golf and lots to do, it's not far from the beach, so we can all walk down and have a picnic on one of the days". "Right, now all of you listen", he said. My heart sank. Here comes the bad news, I thought. We never got good news, here we go, I thought. The boys were still chatting to each other about what they were going to do at the beach, what their friends had done on holiday and how they wanted to do the same. Each brother trying to come up with a better idea than the other. None of them listening to dad, who had a slight smile on his face but soon changed to annoyance when the boys would not stop talking. He said again, "Listen, ALL OF YOU". The boys very quickly stopped chatting and looked at him, all three boys were still stood on the sofa, where they had been happily talking and jumping with excitement. I sat on the floor trying to second guess what he was going to say. It can only be bad news, I thought. I was getting more and more anxious, feeling an intense fear and need to pee. I was still sitting and then sat up onto my knees to listen to him, ready to jump up and go to the bathroom when he had finished with the bad news. He waited until all boys were silent and then looked around at us all, then said "You all have to be on your best behaviour from now onwards. Anyone misbehaving or anyone getting into any trouble from now until then, and I WILL cancel it, do you hear me? All of you, think on, you need to behave". Looking down to me he then said "Right pissy arse, you need to sort out this pissing in the bed or you'll have to stay here. I can't pay for a holiday and then have to pay for the bed you ruin, so think on, if you want to come with us you need to sort it out". He was stood over me, a stern, determined look on his face. "You're the only one that still pisses the bed like a baby. If you need a nappy and rubber pants then fine, if not, then you need to stop it. I MEAN IT, no more, wet bedding from now on or you can stay here on your own. I'm not having you showing me up with your filthy habit, so think on", he said. I was fighting back the tears, mum, the boys and Lucy all looking at me with disapproving looks. I felt the humiliation inside of me, growing like a heat wave. I knew this was too good to be true. I was convinced I would keep myself awake that night and every night until the holiday. I was going to stop wetting the bed, even if it meant I never slept again.

He stepped away from me and leaned over the chair to pick up his jacket, leaning over to kiss Lucy again on her forehead, then said, "Go on upstairs to the loo, you don't want to be a pissy arse like Eddy, now do you?" Lucy just looked up at him and smiled, jumped off the chair and skipped out of the room. I could hear her footsteps banging up the stairs to the bathroom. I stayed sat on the rug as if I hadn't heard his cruel remark. All the excitement now gone from me, I was now worried. What happens if I fell asleep and wet the bed when we got to the caravan? Oh no, I will get into so much trouble. It's not going to be easy to hide it in a caravan. I knew this because I had been on holiday in a caravan last year with Auntie Pam and Uncle Peter. They had put a plastic sheet on the mattress just in case, but just like every time I stayed over at their house, I hadn't wet the bed. I was worrying more and more, just because I didn't wet the bed last time, doesn't mean I won't wet the bed this time. "Up to bed you lot, come on let's be having you" she said, "Eddy, toilet and throw your dad's dirty clothes down out of the bathroom for washing will you? Boys get to bed and stop the shouting or no one will be going on anywhere". The noise from the boy's room seemed to go quiet for a few minutes but then the giggling started up again. She didn't seem to mind, she just stood at the bottom of the stairs. I threw all the clothes down the stairs as she had asked, then went to

75

the toilet. As I sat I was thinking about the holiday, would I be able to go the whole week without wetting the bed. Which bed would I be sleeping in? I couldn't feel happy about this holiday, I was feeling more and more nervous the more I thought about the holiday. I made my way across the landing to my bedroom, opening the door I could smell the stench of urine from my 'filthy habit'. I jumped up onto Lucy's bed and opened the window. If Lucy came up to this smell, she wouldn't be very pleased, she would be shouting her disgust from the top of her lungs and I would be in trouble again. I didn't want that to happen, he hadn't yet left to go to work and they were all happy, I was not going to be the one to end this happiness that enveloped the house this night. I crept into mum and dad's bedroom, slowly walking around the big double bed to the dressing table at the other side. As I passed the window at the bottom of the bed I ducked down so no one outside could see me. I reached the dressing table and reached to the back near the mirror to get the spray. I grabbed it and then started to creep back the way I had just come. I just reached the bottom of the bed and I could hear someone coming up the stairs. I was crouched down at the bottom of the bed, under the window. I froze to the spot. I then heard her bedroom door open, I could feel my heart beating faster in my chest and I held my breath. I was shaking, thoughts running through my mind, what will I say, when asked what was I doing. I let go of the spray and let it roll under the bed. Just as I had let go of the spray the door closed again and I heard her running back down stairs. I let out a loud and long breath. I quickly moved from the bottom of the bed and to the door, I stood with my head to the door, listening to make sure she was definitely gone. Once I was sure the coast was clear I held the handle and quietly opened the bedroom door and then ran from their bedroom back into my bedroom. I stood with my back to the door, panting my breath, I sounded like I had just run a marathon I was gasping for breath. I pulled back my bedding to reveal stained bottom sheet with a wet centre but the outer area of the stain was almost dry. I had wet the bed last night but had told her I hadn't so didn't get to change my bedding as she was up early this morning and I had no time alone to change the bed and put my dirty bedding in the wash without her knowing. I pulled the sheet to one side and then tried to get into the bed and lay on my side in the dry part of the bed and out of the cold, wet, smelling patch. This was not the first time and would not be the last time I would have to do this. I had settled into the bed thinking about how I was going to stop myself from going to sleep. I was trying to think of ways to stop me from wetting the bed from now until and during our holiday.

"Oh my god, it's freezing in here, MUUUUUM, Eddy's been hanging out of the window, it's still wide open and she is pretending to be asleep", shouted Lucy. It was very late now, it was pitch black outside, but with the bedroom light on, my eyes started stinging in the light as I woke up and looked towards Lucy. When I eventually came round I realised my error. Despite my attempt at staying awake all night, I had forgotten to close the bedroom window before getting into bed and then gone to sleep. "Just close the bloody window Lucy and get into bed will you? And, stop shouting or you will wake the little ones up", said mum. "But its freezing in here now, you expect me to sleep in this cold? You should try sleeping in it", shouted Lucy, she was getting more and more angry. As she jumped off her bed after closing the window she kicked the mattress on my bed. She knew I was awake but I kept my eyes closed, pretending I was still sleeping. "I hate you, you're just a dirty, smelly, little bitch. Wait until I tell my dad in the morning, then you will know about it and I am warning you, if you stink my room out again I'm going to go living with gran", she whispered to me, her breath on my cheeks. I was listening to her and thought how good it would be if she did go and live with gran. Being able to have a room to myself and not have to listen to her moaning about me all the time. No one to tell on me when I had not been able to wake up in the night to use the toilet. I lay daydreaming of how nice it would be if she were to go living with gran. I soon drifted back off to sleep.

Chapter Seven

We were all sat in the back of the Bedford van he had made into a makeshift minibus. Seats across the sides of the van, we all sat in the back with him and her in the front. We had all our cases piled up on the floor in the middle of us all. One of the bags was sliding about and kept hitting the side of my leg. As I tried to move to the right of me to get away from the moving cases, Lucy shouted, "Muuuuum, will you tell her, she's pushing me". She moved towards me and pushed her elbow into my ribs. "Ouch, you didn't have to do that, Mum, she just hurt me" I cried. "Eddy stop messing about or I will be the one hurting you, now keep bloody still and stop bloody whinging will you" she shouted. As I sat back, rubbing my ribs, staring at Lucy. "If I have to stop this van and come to sort you out, young lady you will know about it", he shouted. I knew he was directing the threat to me, he never raised his voice to Lucy. I snivelled and as hard as I tried I could still not hold back the tears. "Daaaad, she's whinging now, pissy arse the mard arse" said Lucy whilst smiling a half smile at me. The boys then joined in and within seconds they were all chanting, "Pissy arse the mard arse". Eventually after about five minutes of this, Lucy and Peter had stopped chanting but Luke and Jimmy continued, giggling with every word. "Ok that's enough now, quit it" she said. "I'm telling you now, I'm not going to be sitting in a caravan listening to that whinge for a week. You'd better sort it out", he said. I knew exactly who he meant. I don't know what I had ever done to him. I can't remember a day when he even pretended to like me. It was as if he had just instantly disliked me and I no matter how hard I would try or how nice I would try to be, offering him cups of teas, getting his slippers, he never thanked me or kissed me on the head like he did when Lucy did any of the tasks. Which was rare, she didn't do anything if it meant doing something for someone else. If anyone asked her to do anything her usual response was, "what did your last slave die of?" She always got away with it and then I was shouted to do the task she had blatantly refused to do. I moaned about this maybe once or twice but then got a slap for back chatting.

We arrived at the camp site. I was excited and happy, but needed to use the toilet. If I asked for the toilet the chanting would start so I kept it to myself. I was bursting to pee. He drove slowly into the camp site and over the bumps to park outside the reception cabin. He parked up and got out of the can. "Sit still, you lot, I will go and get the key and directions to the caravan". I was now even more desperate to use the toilet but still I couldn't ask. Lucy jumped from the seat as he left the van, "I need the toilet, dad, can I come in with you? "Come on then love, but you lot sit still and wait until we come back". "I need the toilet too, I'm bursting", I shouted. "Oh Eddy for god's sake, sit down and let him get the key for the caravan, you can go when we get in the caravan, always wanting to do what Lucy's doing, that's your trouble". I sat rocking on the seat, not sure if I was going to pee myself or if I would be able to hold it in until we got to the caravan. Again this upset me and my eyes began to fill up with tears. I turned to look out of the window so the boys couldn't see me getting upset. I held in the tears, not sure if I was going to be able to hold the wee and tears. As the minutes passed by, my urge to pee was getting stronger and stronger, until Lucy came out of reception with him and then I could hear her shout. "Look, ice cream, can we have an ice cream, oh please?" She was holding his hand and pulling him away from the van towards the ice cream van. "No love, let's go and find the caravan and then we can come back for ice cream when we have had some dinner". Reluctantly she stopped pulling him and with a sulk she started to walk over to the van and go back in, climbing over the cases to sit back behind the driver's seat. Leaning on me as she was passing and pushing me slightly to one side, I was sure I was not going to be able to hold in the pee. He got in the front and started to drive around the camp site, bump after bump, lines and lines of caravans, until eventually, Jimmy shouted, "there, there, it's over there, number 42, the green one". He drove over one more bump and to the side of the caravan. The van doors flung open and the boys all jumped out, Lucy pushed passed me again to get out of the van. I was still trying to stop myself from peeing. As I eventually stood to get out of the van, I could feel I had wee'd a little. I got out of the van and walked towards the caravan door. I got in and then made straight for the toilet. "Oh come on Eddy, go and help with the cases first". He said. "Let her go to the loo first, or she will be pissing herself" she said to him.

"Can we go swimming dad?" said Lucy. "Yeah, let's go swimming" shouted Jimmy, running back into the small bedroom he had taken his case into. Peter and Luke were jumping on the beds singing, "We're all going on a summer holiday, no more worries for a week or two" giggling and singing at the top of their voices. "Stop with the noise now boys, you're giving me a headache", she shouted above them all. The singing instantly stopped and the caravan went quiet. "Aww daaad, can we go swimming, pleeeaase?" moaned Lucy. "Lucy shut up and stop mithering your dad, he's driven all the way down here and now it's time we had a cup of tea and your dad had a sit down". She said. Lucy just stared at her, she was not happy about this. He stood up and walked past Lucy ruffling her hair on his way past. "We'll go tomorrow Lucy; don't worry we've got all week". He walked into the small toilet room and closed the door. Lucy stamped her way across the caravan, every step made a noise and made the caravan move slightly, she sat slumped on the sofa with her back to us all, she was looking out of the window. "Oh put your face straight Lucy, like he said, you can go in the morning, it's not all about you, you know", she said. He came out of the toilet and raised his voice at her. "Ok, Ok, leave it now, she knows, you don't have to keep going on about it women, for Christ sake". He walked across the caravan, turned on the TV as he walked past it and then sat next to Lucy. "Do us some tea will ya?" he said.

"I was thinking we could go and have a drink in the camp bar tonight. Lucy can look after the little ones, can't you love and If they don't behave then they won't be going anywhere tomorrow, except home", he threatened. "We'll behave", said Jimmy "won't we," he shouted to Luke and Peter who just nodded heads. Lucy quietly said, "Oh great holiday this is going to be for me, babysitting these lot while you two get to go out and get drunk. Brilliant". She kicked off her pumps and they landed near the caravan door. "Oh give it a rest Lucy, and take your shoes off properly, I won't tell you again, you need to get used to doing as you're told young lady" she said. Lucy then stood tall and as she was stamping across the caravan towards the door, she shouted, "Some holiday this is turning out to be, I hate you, why you had to keep having kids when you don't want to look after them, I will never know". By this time, she had her pumps back on and she opened the caravan door and walked down the flimsy aluminium steps and slammed the door closed. She was stood looking at him, "You going to let her get away with speaking to me like that? The cheeky little bleeder, I've had just about a bellyfull of her cheek". "Oh give it a bleeding rest women, is it any wonder she gets pissed off with you, you never give up. Try listening to her instead of barking orders at her all the time. You stay here, I will go and get her". "Oh you do that and make sure she doesn't speak to me like that again, will ya?" Up he got, slipped his shoes back on and walked out of the caravan, shutting the door behind him, the caravan shook again. She stood in the kitchen area, unpacking the shopping she had brought with her. She was muttering under her breath. "Right Eddy, make yourself useful and put the kettle on and make me a brew". I didn't argue, I just got up and did as I was told.

We had all sat and eaten tea, around the table in the caravan. I was washing up the dishes and Jimmy was trying to dry them. He could only just reach the draining board but it was his turn. She came out of the bedroom, wearing a lovely navy skirt, tan tights and a pale blue blouse. She had done her hair and make-up in the double bedroom in the caravan whilst he slept on the bed. She had woken him about 20 minutes ago and he was now in the small bedroom getting dressed. He walked into the open area of the caravan, looked at Lucy with a big smile and said, "Will I do?" Lucy then stood up on the sofa and said, "Come here, your shirt needs sorting at the back". He did as he was told, stood whilst she put his collar straight, he then turned round and kissed her on her forehead. "Well, am I the most handsome man you have ever seen?" he said as he was looking at himself in the mirror over the electric fire. No one answered him, as he stood patting his aftershave onto his cheeks and chin. She came and stood by his side, holding her small black shiny clutch bag that matched her shiny black stilettos. "Right now, you lot", she said as she was walking towards the small bedroom where all the boys were pretending to be sleeping, squeezing their eyes shut, but giggling at the same time. "I know you are all kidding me, now behave yourselves, do you hear me? Any of you, don't do as Lucy says and you will be in big trouble and no swimming or beach in the morning. You hear me?" All the boys then looked up at her and nodded, Jimmy then shouted, "We will mum, honest, but can we have some ice cream tomorrow and hot dogs too if we are really good?" She laughed at him and as she walked away from the bedroom she said, "Well, let's see if you can all behave first". Off they went out of the caravan, the door causing it to shake as it closed. I could hear her shoes click clacking up the path towards the club house.

I was woken by the sound of voices, I kept my eyes as tight shut as I could. They were whispering but not very quietly. My bed was made up of part of the sofa, in the lounge area with Lucy sleeping at the other side. Even on holiday and they can't be friends for more than one day, I thought to myself. "And you thought this was a good idea? To take your family on holiday and then drop this on us? What are you thinking? What have we done to deserve this? Why? Why?" she was sobbing now. He just stood leaning on the sink, over the small fridge, looking at the contents. Not actually taking anything out of the fridge. He then stood up, slamming the fridge door. "We? What do you mean We? What are you talking about woman, you haven't got a clue what you're on about". I stayed very still, my eyes shut tight. He then walked towards the fireplace and picked up his van keys. "You can have your holiday, I've had enough of you, and I'm going home". He walked towards the door, the caravan shaking as he walked. Surely he won't go home, I thought, he won't leave us here, will he? As he slammed the door shut, I heard Lucy shout, Daaaaad, I allowed myself to peep through one eye, Lucy had jumped from under her covers and run towards the caravan door, crying and pulling at the door. Once the door was opened I could hear the engine of the van as it left the parking space right at the side of the caravan. I stayed very still listening to the sound of the van fading away. "Bastard, you dirty rotten Bastard" she said through tears. "Mark my words, this is not the end, I will bleeding kill him and her". She was saying this to herself. My right arm was now tingling and going numb, I had been lying on it and it started with pins and needles, I had no option but to move. As I moved she turned to look at me, "Its ok, you can stop pretending to be asleep, he's gone now, gone to be with his fancy piece". I sat up and rubbed my eyes. She then walked to the caravan door and said, "Lucy come in, you don't want to run after him, yes he left you too, not just me, he left all of us here. His fancy piece obviously means more to him than any of us. He brought us miles away from home to drop this little bombshell. Why? Why? You may ask. Because he's such a nice man". She said in a very sarcastic but tearful tone. Lucy came in and then shouted at her, "What have you done? Why's he gone home? How do you think we are going to get home now? You can't drive, we've got no car. I want my Daaaaad". "Listen to me girl, you don't have a bloody clue, your precious daaa has been having a bleeding affair for months with that floozy from the club and now he's gone and left us, his family, to be with his bit on the side, but when she throws him out, which she will, mark my words and he will come crawling back and expect me to take him back. Well if he thinks it's going to be that easy, then he can think again". She was shouting through tears and broken speech.

Lucy came back in, she was still angry and upset with her. "You just had to cause trouble tonight, didn't you? You couldn't leave it until we got home. Now you have ruined the

86

holiday for all of us. He didn't leave us, he left you". I heard the slap before I realised what had happened. Lucy was now sat holding her cheek in her hand and sitting back on the sofa area she had been sleeping on, just a few minutes earlier. She just sat for a few minutes then got up and walked towards the bathroom at the other end of the caravan. "We need to pull together now and work out how we are going to get home, we can't stay here with no money and no way of getting home. We don't even have the money for the man who rented us the caravan and he is coming for the money on Monday morning. Oh Jesus, what has he done to us? As long as I live I will never forgive him for this". She started to tear up again. Lucy walked past her and sat back in her bed area, holding her knees under her chin, she was sat looking at her knees. I could see the red mark from the slap on her cheek. I had never seen her shouted at before, so this was a shock. It's a good job he wasn't here; he would go mad I thought to myself. No one hurts his princess. Although she would mock and laugh whenever I was slapped or hit, I couldn't help feeling sorry for her. She had not deserved to be slapped, he was the one in the wrong, not Lucy. I stood up and walked across the caravan and filled the small kettle with water and put it on the small stove. I stood back while I struck a match to light the gas. "Take the cap off Eddy and watch for it boiling or the whistle will wake the little ones". I did as I was told and kept myself busy rinsing cups and making tea for us three. We were all sat staring into our tea cups. I was thinking about how this will play out when he comes back to the caravan. Will he be happy or angry, will he be able to find the right caravan? I had walked to the toilets and showers with the boys earlier and they had run off playing hide and seek and it took me ages to find the right caravan. The van outside was the only way I identified the correct one, that and the fact Lucy was sat looking out of the window and pulling her face at me. Would be blame me? Would I get hit when he finds out Lucy has been hit? Will he hit her? My thoughts were interrupted by a noise outside the caravan. We all looked up, Lucy said, "What was that? Eddy stop messing about, you're not funny". Before I could protest my innocence, mum stood up and looked out of the window near the kitchen are said, "Shhhhhh, it's the bloke from the caravan next door, he's just come in from the club house, he must have slipped on the steps, he's pissed. Well at least someone's having a good holiday. Can't say so much for us". She walked back to sit with us on the sofa area and covered her knees and feet with half of Lucy's blanket. "Right the only way we are going to get home is by putting all our money together and buying train tickets". Lucy and I let out a gasp. "Well how else do you think we will get home? You got any other bright ideas? Because if you have, I'd love to hear them". She opened her purse and tipped out the contents onto the cover on her knee. She started to count her money. Lucy then said she had so much money and together with mum's that would get three of us home. We had six of us to get home. I then reached under the sofa bed into my travel bag to get out my purse. I was just about to open it when she took it from my hands. "Pass it here", she said as she started to empty and count out the contents. Now we had enough for 5 of us to get home but not 6 of us. "Do we have to pay for Luke? Said Lucy, "No we're going to leave him here, what do you think"? "I meant like you don't pay for him on the bus". "Oh we might just get away with that" she said, "Good thinking. We just have to make sure he doesn't tell anyone how old he is. Well we can only try, if not we are all stuck here".

We were all walking carrying our bags and trying to drag the cases. She told the boys we were going on a train trip. She did not tell then the holiday was over and they didn't ask, not even questioning why we had packed our bags again or why we were walking in the rain to the train station without him. Jimmy asked where dad was when he first woke up and she told him he had gone out. He never questioned this and the other two boys never asked after him. The boys were giggling and jumping in puddles along the path to the station, all three of them were wet through from the knees down. She kept telling them to stay out of the puddles but they took absolutely no notice. We ended up at the train station, standing under the veranda. She went to the train master's office to get the train tickets. I could see her smiling and laughing at the man behind the counter. She was giggling like a little girl and touching her hair, she stood side on with her back to us. I turned away to look at the boys, they were now standing on the edge of the track bending over looking to one side trying to see if they could spot the next train. "GET BACK OFF THE EDGE, YOU MIGHT FALL OVER". Shouted Lucy. The boys just looked at her and started to laugh, but did as she had said. Mum came rushing back, "You lot, get over here, will you, right I've got the tickets, the train isn't due for another hour and half. You lot need to sit still and wait. We get the train to York, it takes about four hours to get to Manchester". Peter then looked up at her, "Why are we going to Manchester? You said we were going on a train trip". "We are, we're at the train station aren't we"? Peter seemed to understand what was happening. He didn't ask any more questions, he just sat on the floor by the side of the cases. Luke and Jimmy both still oblivious to the fact our family holiday had barely begun and it was over.

The train journey was uncomfortable, we had no seats for the first few stations, the boys sat on the floor but Lucy and I stood next to the cases, propping them up with our legs. My legs were bruised by the cases which kept banging against them. Eventually we got to one station and the majority of the travellers got up and left the train, pushing and squeezing past us to get off the train. My legs were now stinging with the soreness of the cases pushing against them. Finally, we all managed to get a seat, I was sitting near the luggage rack with the big case still leaning against my legs but not hurting now as I was able to move both legs. Lucy and the boys were sat four seats in front of me and she sat one seat in front of them. I found myself day dreaming about our holiday, imaging we were all in the clubhouse dancing to the kid's music with our parents looking on lovingly. We were happy in my daydream, we all danced and laughed and drank fizzy pop and he would bring us all crisps back from the bar. He would shout us all back to the table they were sitting on and give us our crisps and we would be polite and thank him. I jumped as my chin bobbed onto my chest and the train came to a stop. The large lady sitting next to me was standing up and instead of asking me to move she was trying to push past me. I was pressed into the seat by her large hip. Why she could not just let me stand up and let her pass? After what seemed like ages she eventually managed to squeeze herself past me. I took in a gasp of air and then blew this air back out loudly. She just tutted and continued on her way off the train. I looked down the train to the seats where my family were sitting. I could hear two of the boys arguing about who was going to win the next wrestling match. They were planning a tournament for when they got back to the caravan. They still had no idea we were never going back to the caravan. Peter was quiet, maybe sleeping, I thought. The train started to slow down, she jumped up and shouted, "Come on Eddy get that case and that bag, this is our stop". I tried to push the heavy case into the isle and lifted the bag over this. We all carried the bags off the train, struggling with the weight of them but managed. We must have looked a sight, five young children and a small woman dragging cases that were nearly as big as us. It was around 9pm, it was dark and still raining. We were tired, wet and miserable, but we were nearly home.

Once we got home, the cases were dropped into the front room on the floor. I was told to go make a brew. Lucy ran upstairs to the bedrooms; she was looking for him. He wasn't there, she knew this, just as we all knew, but she had to look. Jimmy was crying, a tired cry, we had had a very long two days and had been through every emotion possible in such a short time. I carried the cups into the lounge, passed one to her and one to Lucy, who was now sat on the sofa in a mood. I went back to fetch my cup of tea, as I walked into the lounge, "Oh I don't think so lady, you'll end up pissing the bed and that's all I need, go and pour that down the sink and get yourself and that bag of yours up to bed". I didn't argue, I just turned round and then walked back to the kitchen. As I got to the sink, I put the cup to my mouth to have a tiny sip of the tea. The tea was too hot even for a small sip, so I poured this down the sink. I picked up my bag, it seemed to increase in weight, and the palm of my hands were still read and stinging from carrying the bag and dragging the cases from the train station. I put the bag on the floor at the bottom of my bed, took out my nice clean night dress, got changed and got into my comfy bed.

It was Monday morning, the boys were up, I could hear them messing about and arguing in the kitchen. Lucy was fast asleep in her bed next to me. I got out of bed quietly and crept out of the bedroom, being careful not to wake her. I walked across the landing to the bathroom. As I sat on the toilet it all came back to me, the arguing, the shouting, the horrible train journey. I went over to the sink to wash my hands, the water stung my palms, I had blisters that had burst and the skin had peeled back to expose the full soreness. I carefully wiped my hands on the towel. I walked down the stairs and went into the lounge, mum was sleeping on the sofa in the lounge, she hadn't been to bed. I then walked from the lounge, closing the door behind me to stop the noise from waking her. As I walked into the kitchen I took one look at the boys, they had been having a food fight, cornflakes and flour and water everywhere, I gasped as I stood in the doorway. Peter was standing on the kitchen table, with flour all over him and his pyjamas were wet from the water they had been throwing. Jimmy and Luke were both standing on chairs, Jimmy had a full cup of water held over his head and Luke was on the other chair, holding the empty flour bag up in front of his head, as if to shield himself from the water. They all stopped and starred at me standing at the door, I stood with my mouth wide open, what had they been doing? She would go mad when she sees this. At that moment Jimmy threw the water and Luke threw the flour bag at me, I was standing drenched and covered in the remnants of the flour bag, I let out a scream, in shock. I was still standing in the door way trying to register what had just happened, when I felt a sharp heat across the back of my head. She was standing behind me, still looking sleepy and shocked. "What the hell have you lot been doing?" The boys were still giggling. They were trying not to laugh but could not hold it back. Every time one of them stopped laughing one would set of laughing and this would then set them all off again. No matter how much she shouted, they just laughed and laughed. She slapped me again across the back of my head, I was bending over holding my ear and crying at the pain. "You think its funny do you? Well, you three bed, NOW, and you can stay in bed all day", she then looked at me and said, "you get this mess cleaned up now, before I really lose my rag". The boys all still giggling walked past her at the door and tried to duck out of her reach, she caught all three with a slap across the head. This did not stop them from laughing, as they made their way up the stairs the laughter got louder and louder.

I had nearly finished cleaning all the flour and cornflakes and water off surfaces and I was starting to sweep the floor when Lucy came in, she looked at me and said, "Do a brew". I stopped the sweeping and looked up at her, I felt like screaming at her to do the brew herself. She knew this, she also knew I wouldn't say anything. I put the brush down and picked up the kettle, shook this to check it had enough water in and turned on the gas. I continued to sweep the floor, the kitchen now clean, I went to the lounge to see what drinks I was making. Sitting in the lounge was Auntie Nora and Auntie Paula, both sitting either side of the sofa, Lucy was sitting with her feel curled underneath her on the chair and mum was kneeling down in front of the fire. She was relaying the whole holiday episode, from getting to the caravan, to being back home. She was at the part of the argument where they were both walking back to the caravan, from the club house. "I was fuming, so I said, oh right, so you think she wants you, do you? Well we'll see about that, when I get my hands on her". She stopped looked at me and said "Why are you stood there like Piffy on a rock?" she growled at me. "Who wants a brew?" I said. "We all want a brew, idiot, now stop ear wigging and get back in the kitchen". I daren't argue, I just did as I was told, I made four cups of tea. I carried two cups into the lounge, passed one cup to Aunty Paula, "Thanks Eddy Love", she said. The next cup I passed to mum, she looked at the colour of the tea and said, that looks

94

like cat piss, go and put another teabag in and let it brew will you, take Paula's too". "No, no, mine's fine love, honest" said Auntie Paula as she winked at me. I took her cup of tea back into the kitchen. I checked Auntie Nora's cup of tea, it looked ok to me, not like cat's piss at all. I walked back in and passed the cups to Aunt Nora and Lucy, "Thanks", said Aunt Nora. Lucy just looked at me and sucked in her teeth as she held the cup in both hands and the cup burnt her hands. "Idiot, you trying to burn me? Get it and put it on the floor" she shouted at me. "For god's sake Eddy, can't you make a simple brew without causing injury to people?" I took the cup and put it on the floor, as I bent down in front of Lucy she smiled a sly smile at me as I stood up I glared back at her. "Don't be giving me your looks, girl, I'll wipe it right off your face, I'm just in the mood for you today". I looked down and walked back to get mum's cup of tea. She was back in full swing of telling the aunties what had happened and why we were all back home so soon after going on holiday. I left the room and went to the bedroom to get changed out of my nighty that was dried with flour and water stuck to me. I walked past the boy's room, they were all sleeping. They must have been up early this morning to cause all that mess.

I sat on my bed, I could hear her voice, she was shouting, telling the aunties how she had shouted at him and what she had told him she was going to do. Lucy came into the bedroom and got back into her bed. The room was cold, the windows had condensation running down them and mould on the wooden frame. Our bedroom was at the back of the house overlooking the back garden. You could only see the garden and the rear of the house on the next street. Lucy's bed was under the window, she had teddies on the bottom of her bed and a very nice pink candlewick top cover. I had an old one gran had given us a few years ago, mine was green and it had small bits of the pattern missing. Lucy had a dressing gown in this material too. She looked nice and toasty warm wrapped up in her bed. I was still sitting on the bed. I had a blue elasticated waist skirt on and a black t-shirt on with a green cardigan. All clothes that used to belong to Lucy, as she got bigger or needed new clothes I would get her old clothes as I was younger and smaller than her. I didn't mind this so much, it was when I went out or to school and people could recognise my clothes as previously being worn by Lucy. She would never be very discreet about this. If I saw her in the street when she was with her friends, or went near to her to speak with her she would make a point of telling anyone who would listen that I had her old hand me downs on. She seemed to think this was funny and she would spend time mocking me and laughing with her friends. I avoided her most of the time but if she had left home before me, I was sometimes given a message to pass on to her, which meant I couldn't avoid her.

Other than going to school, I didn't get much chance to go out and play. Every night after school I had my jobs to do. I would have to make sure our bedroom was cleaned, the potatoes were washed and peeled. Even when I had done most of my jobs, she would usually find me something else to do before I could go out to play with my friends. The times I managed to do my jobs and any other jobs she found for me,

I would only be allowed to play outside the house. My friends could be playing anywhere on the estate. They all had set times to return home for tea and then after tea they would all meet up again and have a set time to be home before bed. She was strict with me; I could go out odd occasions but I was told to stay where I could be seen. If I wanted to go and spend time with a friend in their house, even a house on our street, I would have to ask and most occasions that would remind her I was around and she would find something else for me to do, then I would not be able to go and play. If I wasn't doing jobs, or running errands to the shops or passing on messages to any of our aunties then I was sat in my bedroom, either looking out of the bedroom window or sitting on the bed reading. If I was in trouble I would be grounded and have to do all the jobs, not just mine, I would have to do the boys' jobs and Lucy's jobs too. I would not be allowed to go and spend time reading in my room unless she had gone to visit one of the aunties or if they were round and I had made them all a brew and was told to make myself scarce.

Sitting in class, I was day dreaming again, I was far away, I can't remember where, I just know I spent a lot of time sitting looking out of the window and day dreaming when sitting in class whilst the teacher would be speaking. "Well, Edwina, what did I just say?" I jumped out of my dream state and turned to face Miss Rigby, my school teacher, a small thin lady, very pleasant who spoke with a nice posh accent. She always wore very colourful scarves. Today she was wearing a yellow and blue scarf and when you got close enough to her you could see the picture of blue birds on a yellow background. I liked Miss Rigby, I didn't like it when she raised her voice though, she had a very high pitched voice and it would sound like a screech and she would go all red faced when she was cross. "Well if you have got something better to be doing Edwina then please, don't let me stop you, or have you come to school to learn?" My cheeks began to feel flushed as she addressed me. I looked down at the desk. "Don't look away from me, when I am asking you a question," she shouted in her screeching voice. She was really mad now, I didn't have a clue what she had asked me, so had no way of knowing the answer. I just sat silent whilst she shouted. "Right for those of you who think you don't have to listen to me, because you know it all, then please, leave my class room and let's stop wasting our time." No one moved, I think most of us stopped breathing for a few seconds. She very rarely got cross but when she did she was scary. "Ok so everyone is happy to stay and listen. Right then I'll repeat my last question. Has everyone brought in the ingredients for the baking lesson this afternoon?" My heart sunk, everyone in the class seemed to answer with a joyful, and resounding, YES MISS RIGBY". "Hands up those of you who DON'T have your ingredients. You will be going to sit in Mr Burrows' class and I want a note from your mother telling me why you haven't brought your ingredients, as you were informed last week. You have had long enough to get this arranged. I slowly put up my hand, I just wanted to disappear, I had asked her for the ingredients last week and she had said, "Oh for god's sake Eddy, you've got a bloody week before you need all that, stop mithering me and just remind me the day before". I knew exactly what that meant at the time but didn't want to believe it so I just left it at that and then yesterday morning I reminded her of this conversation, "Don't forget I'm baking tomorrow and Miss Rigby said we need all these ingredients". I passed her the paper I had jotted the ingredients on. "Oh she did, did she? And is she going to pay for it? No, I didn't think so, well, I don't know if we have enough money to get this lot, I will have to see later, you can ask Auntie Paula if she has any flour because I don't have any left after Lucy took the last bag for her bloody baking lesson. They ask you to bring it all in but never send you home with any. Costing good folk, a bleeding fortune, bet she thinks your fathers Rockerfella". That was it, I knew it, if Auntie Paula didn't have the ingredients then I would be going to school again with nothing. I had been in this position more times than I want to remember. This time, Tina, one of the other girls was putting her hand up to speak with Miss Rigby. "Miss, Miss?" I looked at her shocked, she never forgot anything, Tina always had the right dinner money, a chocolate bar for lunch and full packed lunch box and sweets. She was a pretty girl, blue eyes and red long curly hair, she wore in a neat plait with curls left hanging down the side of her cheeks and a thick straight cut fringe. "What is it Tina" said Miss Rigby. "My mum said we didn't have enough flour this morning, so she's gone to the shops and she will bring my ingredients and my basket to reception at lunch time". With a big proud smile on her face she then looked at me as Miss Rigby said. "Well Edwina, where is your basket and ingredients?" I didn't need to speak, I just looked up and I could feel tears burning the back of my eyes, I was so embarrassed, why me? Why do I always have to be the one that all the class looks at me with mock sympathy? They were all used to this scenario, it was nothing new for me to be sitting out of an activity due to not having the ingredients or the money for a trip. I had turned up for school two weeks ago on harvest festival day, All the children in my class had brought in a bag with food stuff in, even Benjamin brought in a tin of fruit, his family didn't have much money and he was one of seven children. I turned up with nothing, I was lucky to get to school that day, as they were arguing in the kitchen, I had asked the night before if we had anything for the harvest festival. I wish I hadn't asked, "What do you think it is? Gift week, Charity begins at home, I can't go feeding all the bleeding neighbours, if Miss Rigby wants to feed the street then tell her to be my guest and put her hand in her pocket, now piss off mithering me". Miss Rigby must have been fed up with me, every week I let her down in one way or another. I really liked Miss Rigby and was hoping I could just go into the kitchen in the morning and just take a tin out of the cupboard. She wouldn't notice. Oh but as luck would have it, she was standing in the kitchen all morning, she was arguing with him. She was angry and when she was angry she would be cleaning up, she was wiping the table and washing up at speed whilst shouting at him. "Get out, from under my feet" she shouted at me as I walked past to get a cup of water. I left the house with nothing again.

Miss Rigby looked at me and then round the class

room, "has anyone else forgotten their ingredients?" No one answered. "Right then Edwina, after dinner, go straight to Mr Burrows' class he will have your name on his register. Come see me before home time and I will give you a letter to take to your mum. This can't keep happening". I just looked up at her, swallowing my tears and my pride.

I walked home from school, it was round a corner and across two small quiet roads and down to the end of the street. My school was a small village school, all the children came from the local neighbourhood. Everyone knew each other. The parents that came to the playground to collect their children when school is over, all stand in the playground chatting. It's a very close community, I would walk through the playground on my way home and would say hello to many of our neighbours. Some neighbours would just say, hello, some would ask after family members, "Hiya Eddy, how's your mum doing?" "She's fine thank you Mrs Turner" I would reply. "Can you ask her to call round when she gets a minute please love? I've got her catalogue order at my house". I would nod and continue on my way home.

It had started to rain just before the final school bell rang. I was going to get wet, it had been dry this morning, a bit cool but dry, so I had left for school with just a cardigan on for warmth over my orange and pink checked dress, knee socks and my red sandals. I pulled my cardigan over my head and set off running through the playground to make my way home. I ran up the street and across the first road. Just before I got to the second road I stopped running, panting for breath. I had stopped at the side of Lucy, who was stood waiting to cross the road with Trisha and Janice, two of her class friends. Lucy was standing under her umbrella, with Trisha stood by her side, both shielded from the rain. I watched the cars go past and then set off to walk across the road with everyone else. I just about reached the kerb at the other side of the road and I tripped, missed my footing and fell over the kerb. As I fell my elbows hit the concrete as I had still been holding my cardigan over my head. I let out a scream, the pain in my elbows and knees was excruciating. I lay flat on my tummy for few seconds. One of the mums tried to lift me up but as she moved me I screamed. Then a dinner lady, Miss Bowker came and held me under the armpits and lifted me up. "Come on love, you will be ok, it's just a trip, you'll be ok". I stood up still crying, Lucy and her friends had carried on walking, I looked up and they were at the end of the street just turning the corner. My knees were grazed with grit in them, blood dripping down my legs. My elbows were cut and blood on my cardigan and holes in my cardigan sleeves. Miss Bowker stood over me with her umbrella, shielding me from the rain, she walked me to the corner of the street. She lived on the street opposite to ours. "Right love, you ok going home now? Do you want me to walk you to your door"? I was still crying, I looked up at her and shook my head, "I will be fine now, thank you" I said I then turned away and started to walk home now getting even more wet, tears and rain streaming down my face, my elbows and knees stinging with every single step I made. I got to the gate and had to try to straighten my arm to lift the latch, this sent more pain into my elbow, I cried a bit more. I walked slowly down the path. Knocked on the front door. I could hear shouting, I knocked again. I could see through the frosted glass on the door, someone was coming down stairs. It was Lucy, I knocked on the door again. Lucy walked into the kitchen and closed the kitchen door. Surely she saw me, I thought and if not she must have heard me. Just then I banged on the glass harder, just as I banged the lounge door opened and mum leaned forward and grabbed the latch on the front door, she pulled the door open and shouted, "All right, less of the bleeding banging, I heard you, get in, where the hell have you been?" I was still crying, my elbows and knees were stinging. She didn't even notice, she walks towards the lounge and said, get sorted and then start to wash the pots and do the potatoes for tea, chip them too". I set off trying to walk up the stairs. I took my time, every bend of my knees caused the pain to sting even more. I got to the top of the stairs and Lucy came running up the stairs and pushed past me. I screamed as my right elbow hit the wall. "Oh shut it mard arse and get out of the way, you're filthy", said Lucy as she walked into our bedroom and slammed the door shut. That was my indication I was not allowed in my own bedroom. So I turned and walked towards the bathroom. I passed the boys' bedroom, Luke and Jimmy were both fighting on the bed, they didn't even notice me walking past. I went into the bathroom and closed the door behind me. I put the toilet lid down and sat on the lid. Trying to take off my cardigan whilst trying not to let the wool touch my broken skin area. "Ouch, ouch, oooh," I cried as I moved slowly. Once I had the cardigan off I then looked at my knees, looking at them made me cry even more, I had small pieces of gravel stuck in my knees. The blood had dried on my knees and dripped down my shins. I couldn't bring myself to wipe the knees clean as I knew this would sting even more. I took off my sandals and knee socks then I managed to take off my dress, pulling this over my head being careful not to catch my elbows with the dress. I was standing in my knickers and vest. My vest was an old discoloured white and was wet down the front. I walked out of the bathroom and made my way to our bedroom. As I opened the door and walked in Lucy pushed the door back into me, I screamed as the door made contact with my left knee. "Get out, I'm getting changed. MUMMMMM, will you tell Eddy, I need to get changed and she keeps running in and out of the bedroom". I leaned over and picked up my nighty off the bottom of my bed, I just made it out of the room as she pushed the door shut on me. "Eddy, get down here and do the spuds, I won't tell you again".

I had just finished peeling the potatoes, the door to the kitchen flew open, "you still bleeding doing them, come on, get a move on we want to eat today, not next week". I carried on peeling despite the pain in my elbows. "When you've done that make me a brew and don't take all day about it".

I was skipping down the path, just shouted bye to Kelly who lived up the street. We had walked home from school together. Kelly lived on the next street up the hill from us, she was my age and in my class. Kelly didn't always walk home from school, she used to go to the child minders across the road from school. Her mum was off work this week so we had been walking home together each day. It was cold but we skipped using our skipping ropes and raced all the way home. It wasn't much of a race, we would start giggling and then stop to catch our breath and then start skipping again. Whenever we went past any other children we had to stop skipping until we had passed them, the paths were not wide enough for us to skip past them, we'd end up in the road if we did that. We still got home a bit quicker and I liked Kelly, she was a nice girl, not very pretty, she had brown eyes, like me, a mousey coloured hair, like me and big front teeth that stuck out, Lucy would make fun of me, saying "you playing with the class dunce? You should be happy together". Lucy was never nice about any of my friends. It used to upset me and I would argue with her about saying mean things. I stopped arguing and just let her go on with herself. I liked Kelly and that's all that mattered, that's what Auntie Paula said when I was telling her how Lucy's teasing made me upset. "You take no notice Eddy love, you like her and that's all that matters, What Lucy thinks is her business. You're a good girl, just don't get too upset over things love. You need to toughen up Love, don't take everything to heart, Lucy doesn't mean half the things she says and if you start to ignore her when she is saying nasty and mean things then she will stop". I wasn't quite sure if Auntie Paula was right or wrong, I couldn't see Lucy ever being nice or not having a nasty comment to make about my friends or about me. She seemed to enjoy teasing me at any opportunity and she would say whatever she wanted. She used to even swear at me, but would never get caught for this. Even when I told on her, she would deny it and I would get into trouble for telling tales. In the end I just gave up ever telling them anything, it was obvious they were never going to shout or chastise her. Not like they did me.

I got to the front door and as I was about to open it, mum stood looking down at me with a smile on her face. I looked up in anticipation, I can't remember the last time she opened the door for me, what was happening, why was she in such a good mood? "Come on in Eddy love, have I got a surprise for you." I was getting more and more excited, what could she mean, what would my surprise be? It wasn't my birthday. I hadn't done anything particularly nice recently just gone about my daily activities as normal. I was bursting to know. "Go put your bag and skipping rope away and then wash your hands and take off your shoes and come into the lounge". Her voice was high pitched and excited. What had she got for me? I needed to run to the toilet. All the excitement had my bladder twitching, I ran upstairs, threw my school bag and skipping rope onto the floor outside the bathroom, running in, while hiking up my skirt and trying desperately to get seated on the loo before I wet myself. Was this nerves or excitement I thought to myself while sitting and waiting for the pee to come. No matter how long I burst to use the toilet I always end up sitting before my bladder will release the urine. With a sigh, the urine came, I had managed not to wet my knickers. I pulled up my knickers and was just pulling my skirt straight. I thought I heard something, I stopped and listened carefully. What I was listening for I wasn't sure. I stood for a few seconds straining my ears to hear the sound again so I could identify the noise. Nope, I couldn't hear anything now. I finished pulling my skirt straight and then picked my bag and skipping rope up and walked quickly across the landing to my bedroom. I hung my bag and skipping rope over the edge of my bed. We had bunk beds but Lucy didn't like having to climb on top and refused to be penned into the bottom and she made it quite clear she would not be sleeping underneath 'Pissy arse'. So the beds were put down a few years ago. Lucy wasn't home yet, no clothes on her bed and no school bag. I left the bedroom to run down stairs. As I set off running down the stairs, she shouted. "You washed your hands Eddy? Don't come in here unless your hands area clean, dya hear me?" "Yeeessss mum". I shouted with excitement. I turned round and ran back up the three stairs and into the bathroom. I washed my hands and then walked to the airing cupboard at the top of the stairs to get a hand towel to dry my hands on. I threw the towel into the bathroom and watched it land in the bath. I then set off back down stairs. My excitement was building, I had butterflies in my stomach, which made me feel a little sick. I put my hand on the door handle to the lounge, the door flung open and she was standing in the door way, "Come in, come in, look who's here" she said. I stepped further into the lounge. As I saw who was sitting waiting for me, I felt my smile face and the butterflies turned to anxiety and I was sure I was going to vomit. I swallowed down the sickly feeling, I kept swallowing, I then felt an urge to use the toilet again.

He was sitting on the chair, propped up with several pillows, he looked very different, scary, old, small and not like my dad at all. I hadn't seen him since that night, 11 weeks and 3 days ago. He had spent a long time in hospital whilst the doctors and nurses made him better. Lucy and the boys had all been to see him whilst he was in hospital. Lucy had seen him at least once a week in the past four weeks and the boys had all seen him at least twice over the past four weeks. I don't know why I never went to visit him, I just didn't. The noise he made, was a strange sound. He slowly turned his head to look at me. I could see he had a white hankie around his neck, like cowboys on the telly would wear. He was wearing pyjamas and his slippers were placed at the side of his chair. He lifted his hand to his throat and as he did this he pressed on his throat and made a louder sound. I was swallowing back the vomit and working very hard trying not to cry. I was frightened, that night came back to the front of my mind. He didn't look like the man who had pulled me from my bed in a rage. He looked weak and frail but very, very, scary and the noise made him seem more frightening. "Go on then, sit down, what's up with you?" she said. "Don't stand there staring, don't you have anything to say?" Still I stood on the spot as if my feet were rooted to the carpet. I wanted to move, to run but my legs wouldn't move. He put his hand again on his neck and made a noise, nodded to me and his eyes looked like he was trying to smile at me. I wasn't sure if this was a genuine smile or a warning smile. Lucy came running in, rushed past me and straight to him. She jumped onto the chair arm and hugged his right arm. "I knew it, I knew it, I knew when I came down the path that you were home. You all better now dad?" she asked in an excited high pitched voice. He just nodded and then leaned his head forward and kissed her on the back of her head. She kicked her shoes off and they landed on the rug, covered in mud. She didn't say a word, just smiled at her and then said "Eddy make yourself useful and go do us a brew and stop staring, you look retarded stood there". "No change there then", said Lucy and then looked at him who smiled at her attempt at sarcasm. My legs just about moved and I walked into the kitchen. I had just finished the two cups of tea, I walked into the lounge carrying the cups being careful not to spill the tea. I put one on the top of the fireplace and then walked towards him and was just bending down to put his on the floor. "And how do you think he'll reach that?" She said. I stood up again and turned to look at her for direction. Where was I supposed to put it? Lucy jumped from the chair arm and snatched the cup from my hand, causing some of it to spill and burn me. "Oh give it here, idiot, I'll sort it. You can't be trusted to do anything". I was shaking my burnt hand and then putting it to my mouth to blow on the burning sensation from the tea. I stepped backwards until I could feel the chair on the back of my legs. I sat down, still in a state of shock. Why didn't I know he was coming home? Why was this a great surprise? Had she forgotten what he did to me, what he said to me, the last time I saw him? I know I hadn't and the way he was looking at me in a silent stare, made me think he hadn't forgotten either.

The strange noise he was making sounded like wind gushing through the room. I sat chewing on my finger nails, looking over to him but trying not to make it obvious.

It was still dark; the house was silent. I slowly crawled out of my bed and crawled on my hands and knees across the bedroom floor to the drawers at the bottom of my bed, I was being as quiet as possible. The last thing I wanted to do was wake anyone up, most of all Lucy who would make sure the whole house woke up and knew I had wet my bed again. I took out a clean nighty and then crept out of the room across to the landing to the bathroom. I took off my wet nighty and quickly put on my clean nighty. Now I was faced with a dilemma, how do I get back to my room and take off the wet bedding and put on clean and dry bedding without anyone knowing? I leaned on the side of the bath, whilst I listened for any noise. It was quiet, except for his loud gushing noise from his throat. He had to sleep sitting up since he came out of hospital and has to make sure nothing causes the handkerchief and tape to move or dislodge. This would mean he would have to go back to hospital or he may get an infection in his neck. I didn't really understand his illness; I hadn't been told about what his injuries were. I was told he nearly died and that he is lucky to be alive, many times, but never given any more information. He looked small and withered and the noises that came from him made him look more sinister than before. He lifted his hand to his throat and pressed down, as he did this he made a whispery like sound. I couldn't make out what he had said, Lucy just laughed, looked over to me and said, "She always looks like that. Did mum tell you I was going to learn how to play the recorder? I'm already good at it, Mrs Jones said, I should be able to pick up in time for the Christmas carol service. You're going to come and watch me with mum aren't you? Pleeeaasse, all the mums and dads will be there". He nodded and patted her on her knee, looked up and smiled at her. She was glowing, happy he was home. "Come on now Lucy let your dad rest now, come and help me make the tea. Eddy, don't just sit there, go and get the potatoes peeled". I jumped from my seat and walked out of the room, leaving the door open so they could follow me. "Oh for god's sake, was you born in a barn? Shut the bleeding door, do you want him to end up back in hospital? Honestly I don't know where you get your brains from girl. Edddddyy" she shouted. I run back and closed the door.

I sat in the kitchen on the bench with my back to the wall. Jimmy sat beside me, Luke and Peter facing us. Luke was eating his food and making a slopping noise with every bite. The noise was getting louder and louder with every mouthful. He did this on purpose, I was sure. He knew I didn't like this and his eyes were smiling at me as he enjoyed teasing me. He was younger than me but knew this would upset me. I stopped eating and looked directly at him, "Do you have to?" I asked him. He swallowed his food, "Do I have to, what?" he asked with a sly grin, he knew exactly what I meant, he was still teasing me. Jimmy and Peter started to giggle at him. This just caused him to eat making even more noisily. I stopped eating, stood up and walked to the bin to throw my tea away. I couldn't eat any more, the horrible sounds he made when eating made me feel sick. My stomach was now churning; I wasn't quite sure if I was going to vomit or not. Just as I had tipped the plate and scrapped the food into the bin, "What's up with your tea? I stand and cook for you all and you think its ok to just throw it away? Well, no pudding for you lady". She said as she walked into the kitchen just as I had finished tipping away the food. I just stood looking guilty, "Luke kept eating like a pig and made me feel sick". "Oh really? And you thought it would be ok to just throw your tea in the bin? You think we're made of bleeding money and can fork out for food for you to tip into the bin? Well, let me tell you lady, we don't have money to burn so if you can't eat your tea then you won't be eating any pudding. Now start the pots" she said. "It's Lucy's turn to wash up, not mine" I said. "Well that's hard luck, you shouldn't throw away good food, there's millions starving in other countries and you think its ok to throw a full meal in the bin, now stop arguing with me and wash the pots". I ducked down as she walked past, I was trying to dodge the slap I knew was coming. She caught me, a hard slap that caught my right ear and slightly caught my right cheek, despite my moving. My eyes welled with tears, I tried and tried to hold back the noise, but was unable to hold it in. I sniffed up and then let out a cry, the slap causing my ear and right cheek to sting. She stepped back and started to walk towards the door. The boys all sat up, looked down at their plates and stopped giggling. As she got to the door, she turned to face the boys sitting at the table, "eat your tea, no more messing about or you will all have no pudding and go straight to bed. Dya hear?" They sat in silence and just nodded to her. I was still holding my cheek and leaning against the sink, not wanting to make eye contact with her in case I made her even angrier with me.

I had finished washing the dishes, I walked into the lounge with the towel in my hands as I dried them. "I've washed the pots, who's drying them?" I said as I looked at Lucy. "Erm, it's your turn to dry the pots," said Lucy. "Well it was your turn to wash the dishes and I have done them so you can dry the pots". "Muuuuuum, that's not fair, it's not my fault she put her tea in the bin and had to wash the dishes, it's her turn to dry them, you tell her?" said Lucy. "Eddy for god's sake, can't you just do as you're told, you threw away your tea, so now you can wash, dry and put away the dishes, your lazy little bleeder". I looked towards Lucy, she was still sitting near him and they both looked at me with smug smiles, that didn't completely meet their eyes. I was furious and this made me more upset so I turned around, closed the door behind me. I wanted so much to slam the door shut, but didn't dare too. I went back into the kitchen to now dry and put away the pots. I was feeling upset and angry; why did she get away with doing nothing I had to do everything? I stood looking over the sink at the mountain of pots I had now to dry. The boys were still sitting at the table; they were giggling at each other. Food all over the table, Nan was right, it did look like feeding time at the zoo when they all sat together. Jimmy had nearly finished his tea, "get me a drink, Wiff" he said. "Get up and get your own, what do you think I am? Your slave?" I replied. "Yeah I do, now do as you're told or you will have to stay in detention", he said mocking his teachers who would threaten him with detention nearly every day for back chat or bad behaviour. "Look, you can get your own drink, I'm busy". "MUUUUUMMMMM, Eddy won't get me a drink", he shouted. I cringed as I waited for her response. "EDDY, Do the bloody drink will, you, why do you have to be so awkward?" she shouted. "I'm drying the pots; he's finished so he can get his own". I replied. Nothing was shouted back, I was just about to smile at Jimmy to get his own drink when the kitchen door flew open and banged against the wall and swung back into her, as she put out her hand to stop the door from going any further. "And who the hell do you think you are speaking to young lady?" As she said every word she slapped me in time to her words, one slap across my head per word. I was ducking and trying to dodge every slap which just made her rage with anger, but my instinct told me to get out of the way of the slaps. With every single slap I let out a cry. The boys had now gone silent again, not wanting to draw any attention to themselves and cause her to be angry with them. "When I tell you to do something, you do it, I've just about had enough of your lip and wise cracks. Get the bloody drink and then finish the pots, dya hear me? When you've done that you can go and run the bath for the little ones." I was now whimpering like a puppy in the corner of the kitchen between the sink and cooker, as I had tried to move away from every slap but she had just followed me. My head was now hurting even more and my ears were making a ringing sound. She walked backwards out of the kitchen still looking at me and just before she shut the door, she looked at me and said "now either do as you told or I will be back and next time, mark my words, lady, I will give you the best good hiding of your life, I'm just in the right mood for you today, dya hear me?" I nodded my understanding and tried to stand up straight. I must have been holding my breath while she was shouting. When she closed the kitchen door behind her, I let out a long sorrowful, half whimper and half a breath of relief. The boys were still sat watching me. None of them speaking or eating. Jimmy then looked at me and said in a hushed voice, "See, told you, you should have just got me a drink". I knew what he was saying but still I couldn't help feeling this was his fault and not mine. Still I had gotten into trouble and now I slowly lifted the plastic cup off the draining board and made him a drink of juice. Luke and Peter both then asked me to get them a drink. I wasn't going to risk telling them to get their own, so I just did as they asked and passed them the drinks. Once the boys had finished eating they all shouted into the front room for permission to leave the table. She replied to them by shouting back her permission. I continued drying and putting away the pots I had already washed and then began the task of clearing their plates, cups and wiping the table and chairs, washing the rest of the pots and then drying them and putting them away. I found myself daydreaming when I was cleaning up in the kitchen. I often spent time thinking about my life and how it will be when I get older. I will have a nice house and nice husband who will go out to work and provide for his family. We will be happy have lots of family holidays, a little girl who will have nice pink clothes and a little boy who will look after his little sister and love her and protect her. Not like my brothers and sister, not like her or him.

I was in the bedroom changing out of my school clothes and into my night dress as she had told me to do. I had walked home from school in the rain, it was dark now even though it was only 4pm. The winter seemed to have come early this year, black clouds and rain seemed to be all the weather we ever had. I froze to the spot when I heard the whistle, my whole body felt like spiders were crawling over my skin. I felt sick, just the sound could make me feel this way. Then he whistled again. I would try to ignore it and pretend I hadn't heard him sometimes. Not today though, the whistle was loud and he kept whistling, which made me feel a sense of urgency and alarm. I quickly pulled my night dress over my head and ran to the top of the stairs and then shouted "I won't be a minute; I'm just getting changed". Again he whistled and this time it sounded fraught. I was just about to walk back to my bedroom when again he whistled. I turned back around and ran down the stairs. Half way down the stairs and I missed my footing and screamed as I fell down the last four steps, landing with my face on the mat at the door and grazing my knees on the carpet, causing a stinging sore feeling. I began to cry as I landed on the floor. My knees hurt and so did my head, I stayed in this position for what seemed like ages but was probably about a minute. The lounge door opened and Lucy came to look over me,

"Eddy fell the down stairs, she just lay here whinging". "Oh for god's sake, Eddy, can't you do anything properly, get up and stop being such a mard arse, if you looked where you were going, you wouldn't have fallen. Now quit with the noise, I've got a blinding headache and that noise is not helping". I took my time to stand up and tried to stop the crying, stifling the sounds under my breath, the stinging of my knees seemed to increase as I straightened my leg to stand and my forehead felt like I had burnt it. I too had a headache now, and trying to hold in the tears was not helping this. I slowly walked into the lounge to see what he had wanted. What he had been whistling so frantically about. As I walked into the front room they all turned to look at me. "Oh don't come in here and start your bleeding snivelling, you dozy git". I stood for about a minute and then asked. "What did you want me for?" Lucy, dad and mum all just looked at me with puzzled expressions. "You whistled for me, I said I was getting changed but you whistled again and again". They all began laughing at me. Had I said something funny? Did my head look funny now it's grazed, I could feel it smarting along with my knees so no doubt I looked comical to them? Even if I didn't feel comical. I looked at each of them, ending up still looking at him. He grinned at me and then put his hand over his throat and pressed the device he had under the neck scarf and said in a very husky and quiet voice. "No one was whistling for you. Now sod off and take your sorry arse looks with you". It was my turn to look puzzled. I had heard the whistling, I hadn't imagined it, I had shouted I was getting changed. Why did none of them shout to tell me it wasn't me he was whistling at? Then I may not have fallen trying to get down the stairs in a hurry. "What are you still doing there? If you can't find something to do, then go make me and your dad a brew will ya?" That was said, however I was aware this was not a question or request, it was a direct order, so off to the kitchen I went. As I got into the kitchen I sat on the bench at one side of the table and looked down at my carpet burnt knees, still stinging and feeling very tight when I moved my knees. I was sat for about 30 seconds when the kitchen door opened and Lucy came walking in, "Muuuuum, Eddy's just sitting down, she's not brewing up" she shouted. I looked at her in disbelief, wondering why? Why did she have to shout that, I had been sitting for less than a minute, I had just fallen down stairs, why must she always get me into trouble? "Eddy, just do as your bleeding told", she shouted. "Mum said when you've made a brew you need to start peeling the potatoes for tea for us all and dad is going to have some too so peel a few more spuds". Once she had told tales on me and given me my orders she was gone, back to sit with them in the lounge and leave me in the kitchen. Why can't she do the spuds or the brews? Why do I have to do everything? What is it about her that makes her so precious?

I lay still in bed, I could hear Uncle Matt in the bathroom, he was brushing his teeth. He was the only person I have ever heard brush teeth with so much noise. I opened my eyes and smiled to myself. I liked it here, I felt warm and loved. I moved my legs about the bed and moved my hips from side to side, checking the bed was still dry and to my relief it was. "No, It's bone dry" I would say to Auntie Lucy when she asked if I had wet the bed. I could smell the toast and coffee Auntie Lucy was making in the kitchen. "Matt, get our Edwina up will you, I don't want her toast going cold". I jumped out of bed, just as I heard uncle Matt say, "right oh, we wouldn't want her to have cold toast, now would we?", he said with mock sarcasm. I ran to the bedroom door just as Uncle Matt was about to open the door. "Morning", I sang to him. I loved Uncle Matt and Auntie Lucy, they were strict, had lots of rules in their house but once you knew the rules, everything was nice. I would get to go and spend overnights with them every once in a while. "Oh my giddy aunt, you made me jump out of my skin then", said Uncle Matt, laughing at me. He leaned into me and patted me on my head and said "Good morning beautiful, and how did you sleep?" I walked past him and into the bathroom, I was bursting to wee. I shut the bathroom door and raised my voice to answer him. "I had a lovely sleep, thank you". His voice was then fading as he walked down stairs, "Your aunt Lucy has done your toast love, so be sharp and come down and don't forget to wash your hands". I sat on the loo, nodding. I quickly washed my hands and then ran down the stairs and into the kitchen. Auntie Lucy was standing, facing the worktop and buttering the toast she had already made. "Come now, sit yourself down and eat your toast sweetie, help yourself to jam or lemon curd", she said smiling at me. Matt get her a drink of squash, she ordered. He looked up at me from his newspaper, stood up and walked towards the sink, he got the orange squash from under the sink and went about making me a glass of squash. He then walked back to the table and passed me the glass, sat back down and unfolded his newspaper and shook it straight and started to read again. Aunt Lucy came over to the table, with a plate full of toast. The jam, lemon curd, butter and pot of tea, milk and sugar bowl all set out in the middle of the dining table. My heart was always smiling when I was here, I loved my Auntie Lucy and Uncle Matt so much, I used to make believe they were my mum and dad whenever I stayed here. They had called to our house last night after they'd both finished work. Auntie Lucy worked for the labour exchange and Uncle Matt worked for a big company and was very high up and intelligent, they both were. They didn't have any children of their own, they would call to our house and ask if I would like to go and stay over with them for the weekend. I would burst with happiness when they came round, waiting patiently for them to ask me the question. I would instantly jump up and say, "Yes please, please mum can I? I will be good, honest". "We'll have you been a good girl?" asked Uncle Matt. "Yes, yes, I have haven't I mum?" I would ask her to make sure. She would just nod, "you can go but make sure your bed is made, your dirty clothes are put in the basket and make sure you behave or you'll have your dad to answer to." I felt all fuzzy inside, I had butterflies, I was filled with excitement. I ran upstairs, tripping twice on my way up. "Be careful Edwina, or you will be going to stay in hospital for the weekend if you fall downstairs, you dozy duck", shouted Uncle Matt. I just giggled and ran into my bedroom, made my bed, picked up my dirty clothes, walked to the bathroom to put them in the linen basket. "Eddy don't forget to pack an overnight bag and don't forget your clean knickers and socks", mum shouted. I hurried about getting my clothes together, I then ran back down stairs, got a carrier bag out of the drawer in the kitchen and then back upstairs to put in the clothes in. I skipped back down the stairs, Jimmy ran past me, knocking me on his way upstairs, I knocked him back with my bag. "Move Eddy, I need the toilet", he said as he rushed to the bathroom.

Once I was ready I was warned again not to give any cheek and to behave or I would be in trouble. "Oh stop your worrying, she will be fine, she's good as gold for us," said Uncle Matt. "Come on love, get into the car, mind you don't put your mucky feet on the seats or I'll have your guts for garters". I got into the back seat of the car and sat smiling. Mum was still chatting to Auntie Lucy. They stood for few more minutes, Uncle Matt had got into the driver's seat, put on his seat belt and put the key in the car. We sat in silence for a few more minutes until Auntie Lucy got into the car, "ok then see you Sunday after dinner", she said to mum who just nodded to her. She stood looking into the car and waved us off as we drove off the close. As we turned the corner I felt myself let out a breath of air. I wasn't aware of this until Uncle Matt said, "Well that's a big sigh for such a little lady". I just giggled and smiled back at him through the rear view mirror. We drove in silence for about three minutes until we got to Auntie Lucy and Uncle Matt's house. Even though we lived on the same estate, I never saw any of them unless they called at our house. I sat still until Uncle Matt opened the car door and told me to get out. I stood holding his hand then we crossed the road and into the house. We took off our shoes at the front door, took off our coats and put them in the cupboard behind the front door with all their other coats, shoes, boots and wellington boots. This room had hooks along the walls with coats, umbrellas, a small sink on one wall and shelves on the other wall, a row of nail varnish of all different colours on a shelf. The shoe polish and sewing kit was placed on another shelf all in order. Everything in this house had a place and nothing was ever out of place. This house was clean and warm and very homely. I then walked into the lounge with Uncle Matt. Auntie Lucy went into the kitchen and started to prepare our tea. I sat on the sofa and Uncle Matt sat on his chair, Auntie Lucy had her chair at the opposite side of Uncle Matt's with a lamp and small table with an ashtray and bowl of imperial mints on it, in between the chairs. The sofa was side on to the chairs and the TV was facing in a corner and a large speaker in the other corner. They had lots of pictures on the walls, pictures of all the family, pictures Uncle Matt had taken with his camera. They had a very nice black and white picture in a frame on top of a dark side board that covered most of the remaining wall, of them both on their wedding day. Auntie Lucy looked like a princess and Uncle Matt looked very handsome, this was my favourite picture of them. Everything looked brand new here, nothing seemed to ever change or get dirty. Uncle Matt sat back in his chair, lit a cigarette, looked over to me and asked, "What have you been up to in school today? You learn anything interesting?" I shook my head and shrugged my shoulders, "nothing", I replied. He smiled and winked at me, then said "you mean you spend all day in school and they don't teach you anything? Does your mum and dad know about this? You go to school every day and they can't tell you anything you don't already know? I wish I was that clever at school, I had to make sure I listened carefully to my teachers so I could remember everything they told me so I had something I could share with my dad at dinner every night. It's a good job he's not your dad he wouldn't be very happy if I had nothing to share with him". I was now giggling with him, he was kidding me, I knew this, as he had told me this tale before. I then remembered something we were learning about in school. "We learnt about the Egyptians, about how they write in pictures and when they die they wrap them in bandages and put them in a casket and then into a pyramid if they are rich they have all their jewels and valuables put into the pyramid for them to take to the next world". Uncle Matt sat listening to me, smiling and nodding his agreement with everything I was sharing, asking me questions and sharing more information about the kings and queens that are famous in Egyptian history. Some of which I had heard at school but Uncle Matt had a way of telling me things in a way I would never forget. He was calm, interesting and easy to listen to and talk to. I enjoyed our chats and I think he did too. He never told me to be quiet or shut up, he was always willing to listen to me for as long as I had something to say. Auntie Lucy and Uncle Matt never had any children, they worked every day in the week and only had weekends off so probably wouldn't be able to look after any children. This suited me just fine, as they would keep coming down and have time to take me with them and spend time with me. Auntie Lucy came in from the kitchen, she was now wearing her apron over her skirt and blouse, she still looked pretty and her makeup never seemed to move. She always had long well cared for finger nails, always painted in beautiful colours. "Do you want bread and butter with your tea?" she asked. "Oh yes, two please love," said Uncle Matt. "Edwina, do you want a round of bread and butter with your tea?" "Yes please", I replied. I could smell the chips cooking, this made me feel hungry now. "You two go and wash your hands and come and sit down for tea", she said. "Come on kid, best do as we're told or she will get cross and you won't like Auntie Lucy when she's cross, her nose gets all screwed up", he joked, winking at Auntie Lucy as he passed her. I jumped up and ran to the downstairs coat cupboard to wash my hands and used the pink hand towel to dry my hands. As I walked into the kitchen Uncle Matt had just finished drying his hands after washing them in the kitchen sink. He went to sit in his chair at one side of the table. Auntie Lucy had her chair opposite him and my chair was in the middle of both of them. Auntie Lucy passed Uncle Matt his meal then put my plate in front of me. Chips, egg and beans, this smelled wonderful, Auntie Lucy was a wonderful cook. I always enjoyed it here, I didn't have to peel the potatoes or chip them. We chatted whilst eating our meal, each one of us having time to talk and the other two sitting quiet and listening. Not like at home when everyone talked over each other unless dad was speaking or mum was shouting. Once we had finished our meal, Uncle Matt always thanked Auntie Lucy for the meal and complimented her on her cooking and I was always expected to follow his lead which I did without thought. Auntie Lucy would then wash the dishes, Uncle Matt would stay in the kitchen and dry the dishes and I would put away the cutlery into the drawer. Uncle Matt would put away all the plates cups, pots and pans, "we don't want you dropping anything", he would say when I offered to dry the dishes and put them away, despite not being tall enough to reach most of the cupboards. It was like going on holiday coming here. I had a whole weekend of no jobs, no shouting or mocking or name calling, it was brilliant and I was living in a dream as an only child of a very lovely pretend mum and dad. I never dared tell them my thoughts, I kept this to myself and just enjoyed the time we had together. I had nearly completed putting all the cutlery away when Auntie Lucy shouted me, "Edwina, come in here love, let uncle Matt sort the dishes out". I looked up at Uncle Matt who looked down at me, nodded and smiled at me as I put down the towel. Auntie Lucy was stood upstairs looking down on me from the landing, "Bath time young lady, I don't know what you have been up to today but you're so mucky, I've put plenty of bubbles in and your towel is on the shelf with a nice clean nighty. Make sure you wash behind your ears and give your nails a good wash if you want them painting after". She walked past me and tapped me on my shoulder as I walked past and into the bathroom. She shut the door behind her and shouted, and don't forget to brush your teeth. I got into the nice warm bubble bath and relaxed into the water.

I skipped down the stairs and into the lounge in my clean nighty. Auntie Lucy was sitting on her chair, with three nail varnishes set out on the table in front of her. One pink, one red and one an orange colour. "Sit down and hold out your hand. If you want your nails doing for the weekend, the sooner we do it the better. Just make sure we take this off before you go home or your mum will have a right go at me". I sat down opposite her and held out my right hand. "Ok then, choose a colour", she said. I chose the pink, the same one she had on her nails, it looked very pretty on her. "You really need to stop biting your nails Edwina, the polish will look so much better when they are long and filed". I nodded in agreement, I will try my best to stop biting my nails, I so much wanted to have nice nails and a nice hands. I sat very still holding out my hand as she painted each nail. Once they were done I sat waving my hands around to help the nail varnish dry. "Don't catch the cushions with your hands love the varnish won't come out of them". I slowed down waving my hands but kept them held out in front of me. Uncle Matt came into the lounge to join us. "What have you done to her? She looks like a statue. Have you put a spell on her?" he said laughing to Auntie Lucy. "Oh behave Matt," she said to him whilst looking up at him and smiling. He switched on the TV and sat in his chair, lit up a cigarette and relaxed back in his chair with a big sigh. We all sat watching the TV. I was tired out, I had cross country today at school and we were running around the local fields, 1500 metres Mrs Cook said we had run. I enjoyed PE most of the time and really enjoyed running around the field, it made me feel like I was free with the wind in my hair. Except today it rained, which made the running more difficult as my feet stuck to the mud with every stride I took and we all ended up covered in mud. We got back to school, changed out of our PE kits before play time and were told to take them home today for washing before next week's PE class. The nice bubble bath had just helped remove all the mud and grim from the running today.

We all sat watching TV together, I was curled up in a ball with my head leaning on the arm of the sofa. Uncle Matt then got up and walked into the kitchen and then returned with two bags of crisps, one bag of salt and vinegar chip sticks and one bag of cheesy puffs. Every time I stayed over, we had the crisps, the same ones, he put them onto the table and walked back into the kitchen. He shouted, "You want a little glass of juice Edwina?", "No thank you", I replied. Auntie Lucy looked over at me and said, "you can have a small one Edwina, I'm sure that won't hurt", I shook my head. I daren't have a drink, I wasn't going to jeopardise my time staying here the odd weekends by wetting the bed. "I'm not thirsty, honest", I said. "Ok, if you're sure?" said Uncle Matt as he walked in with 2 cups of tea he put down on the small table between the chairs. He sat down then leaned forward and picked up the chip stick and threw them at me, "Open them for us, Kid", he said, then picked up the cheesy puffs and opened them took out a hand full and out them back on the table. I handed the chip sticks over to Auntie Lucy, "No thanks dear," she said. I offered them to Uncle Matt who had a mouth full of the cheesy puffs, he shook his head to decline the chip sticks.

I woke up in my nice warm bed, my eyes hurt with the light coming through the curtains, I stretched my arms out above my head and star fished my legs. I was happy, I hadn't wet the bed and I could smell the fresh crisp bedding. Everything was quiet, no noise from outside and no noise in the house. I knew it was early but I didn't know what time it was. I just lay star fishing with my legs and smiling to myself. I loved it here, in my bed in my pretend new home with my pretend new mum and dad sleeping in the bedroom next door. I must have nodded back to sleep. I heard a coughing and woke up again, Uncle Matt was coughing as he did most mornings, a loud hacking cough. He was still in his bedroom next door. I could hear Auntie Lucy moving about downstairs and could hear the sound of music coming from a radio. I pulled the covers off me and jumped out of bed, I slipped my feet into my slippers and ran to the bathroom across the landing. I was just about to wash my hands after having awe when I heard Uncle Matt shouting, "Don't forget to wash your hands little lady". "I won't", I shouted back with a smile on my face. One of the biggest rules in this house was you washed your hands often. After using the bathroom, you washed your hands, before cooking, you washed your hands, before eating you washed your hands, after helping in the garden you washed your hands. This was a rule I knew too well and made sure I always stuck to it. I ran downstairs and into the kitchen to Auntie Lucy, "Good morning Princess, how did you sleep?" I looked up at her and smiled as she kissed me on my forehead. "Like a log", I relied. She just looked at me in a shocked frown. I wasn't sure what I had done wrong,

I sat at the table and put my head down. Just as Uncle Matt came walking into the kitchen, "you and me both kidder", he said. Auntie Lucy looked at him and said, "don't encourage her to talk like that Matt, she's a pretty little girl and should sound and act like one". Uncle Matt looked at me and dipped his head as he was being scorned by Auntie Lucy, he turned his lips upside down and made a sad face and then winked at me. We both just glanced at each other and kept quiet. Auntie Lucy walked over to the table and put a glass of milk in front of me and the toast in the middle and sat down, facing me. We had nearly finished eating breakfast when Uncle Matt cleared his throat, winked at Auntie Lucy who then nodded to him. "Ok, who fancies going on holiday?" I nearly choked on my toast, I started to cough as I felt it go down the wrong hole, Auntie Lucy picked up my milk and held it up in front of my face, "here, drink some of this", she said. Uncle Matt started patting me on my back trying to help me stop coughing. I eventually stopped coughing, my eyes were watering and Uncle Matt said, "I wasn't thinking of going on a holiday to the local infirmary, chew your bloody food child", he said in a stern but concerned voice. "MATT", said Auntie Lucy, "don't you use that sort of language in my house". "Oh give over woman, she scared the life out of me" he said. "That doesn't give you the right to use that sort of bad language and not certainly not in front of a child. Cover your ears Edwina, don't you ever repeat that sort of filthy language". I was now wiping the tears from my eyes, tears that were caused by the coughing. I had now recovered but was trying to remember if I had actually imagined the word holiday. Was he including me in this question or just asking Auntie Lucy, did I just happen to be here? I sat patiently waiting to hear him ask again and see if I was included. "Well?" he said. They both looked at me, Auntie Lucy then smiled at me and said, "Don't look so scared love, you don't have to come if you don't want to leave your mum and dad, we won't mind, you can do whatever you want". I was in shock; I was looking at both of them wondering if my ears were playing games on me. I had tears in my eyes, and a lump in my throat, I couldn't speak for fear of crying. I was so excited, was this a dream, I thought. Will I wake up soon and be back in my cold damp bed with our Lucy lay in the bed next to mine? Nope, it was really happening and I was being asked if I would like to go on holiday without my mum, dad, brothers and sister? Or if I was too scared and would prefer to stay at home. No competition I thought, I just couldn't verbalise this, I was taken aback and feeling happier than I could ever imagine. Still I stood, staring at him, not sure if this was a dream, was I going to wake up and be back at home in my bed with Lucy sleeping at the side of me? I looked around at Auntie Lucy. She was looking down eagerly waiting my response. "Well"? She said. "We need to know if you want to come with us to the caravan. We are going to Wales, a lovely little town and a very nice and clean camp site. They have a park for you to play on, the beach is within walking distance from the caravan and they have ponies and stables on site, you can go pony trekking too". Uncle Matt picked me up and stood with me near our cases. "You have a choice. You can travel in the case or we can let you sit in the back of the car with a blanket and you can get some more sleep if you want? Or we can drop you off at home on our way?" I started to shake my head and hugging Uncle Matt around the neck, I began to giggle. Uncle Matt and Auntie Lucy both started to laugh with me. "I think she wants to go in the case Lucy Loo, can you take out your shoes? Then we can fit her in?" I was still giggling and shaking my head. "Oh no, wait, she wants to sit in the back of the car with her blanket", he said, winking at me and then at Auntie Lucy. Uncle Matt put me down, "Go to the toilet Edwina, see if you can do a little wee before we set off, we won't be stopping for a couple of hours and we don't want any accidents in the car". I ran off to the toilet.

We seemed to be travelling for a long time and still not at the caravan site to begin our holiday. I was starting to feel hungry again. We stopped earlier at a road side to eat our sandwiches, crisps and fruit for lunch. I must have nodded off, as I woke and sat up, uncle Matt looked at me through his rear view mirror and smiled at me, "Hello, sleepy head, look out of your window over there, he pointed to the right side of the car. I looked up eagerly hoping to see the caravan park the play park or the ponies. No sign of any caravans but I could see the sea and the sand and beech filled with people, sun bathing or playing in the sea or with the sand. I had butterflies in my stomach, the excitement causing me to feel instantly nauseous. Uncle Matt noticed the change in my face. "You ok love?" he said. I was nodding but I wasn't being truthful, I felt so ill it came on fast, I was feeling dreadful but didn't want admit it. I just kept nodding my agreement to him. Auntie Lucy looked at me and said, "You look a little peaky love, you sure you're ok"? I nodded again but as I turned my head towards her I could feel my lunch rising into my throat. "Matt, stop the car, she's going to be sick", shouted Auntie Lucy. I jumped out of the car as soon as the door was opened and instantly vomited on the grass. Auntie Lucy rubbing my back and holding my hair out of the way of the vomit, I was bending over, tears in my eyes, but I wasn't crying. I stood up as Uncle Matt handed me a cup with some water in it. "Here drink this", he said. I took the cup, my hand shaking from the vomiting, I sipped the water and then felt instantly better. I looked up at both Auntie Lucy and Uncle Matt who were looking at me with concern in their eyes. I smiled at them, "How long before we get to the caravan?" I asked. Uncle Matt smiled at me, Auntie Lucy took a handkerchief from her cardigan pocket and wiped my face. "You must have needed that", said Uncle Matt, "your colour has come back into those rosy red cheeks, we don't have far to go now, you sure you're ok to drive a little farther?" I nodded and walked back to get into the car. We arrived at the caravan park, a big white gate was being opened by a man wearing blue jeans and a red t-shirt, it looked like a busy caravan park, with a shop at the entrance with a reception to the side of the shop. A row of stables on the other side, a dark brown tall horse was being saddled up by a girl in a pair of muddy black wellington boots a green top and jeans, she had long blonde hair she wore in a plait down her back, she had a pretty and kind looking face. She looked over the car and saw me sat watching her from the back of Uncle Matt's car. She continued to put the saddle and bridle on the horse and smiled a welcoming smile to me. She was talking to the horse and patting his neck. My excitement was growing, I loved horses and could not wait to find out if I would be able to go spend time with the horses and the pretty girl. Uncle Matt had gone into the reception to get the key and directions to the caravan we were going to be staying in. He came out holding a key with a red fob, he held this up to show Auntie Lucy and I that he had the keys to our home for the next week. We set off looking for the yellow flat to identify the area of the site our caravan was parked. Our caravan was number 407, we drove past lot of caravans and then finally found the row that started with 418, "It must be down this one," said Auntie Lucy, we turned down the row and came to stop outside number 407. We all got out of the car and then went into the caravan together to take our first look around. I had a bedroom with two single beds in it, I chose to sleep in the bed away from the window, the one with the pink bed spread. We set about carrying in our cases and Auntie Lucy made some tea for herself and Uncle Matt. "Let's all have five minutes and then we can go and have a look around the caravan park if you like Edwina?" I was sat on the sofa in the lounge area, my legs tucked underneath me as I looked out of the window at a family playing badminton with a makeshift net across from our caravan. I turned to look at Uncle Matt and nodded my agreement.

We had been to the beach for the day, we had drinks, sandwiches and biscuits for lunch, we had a wind break that Uncle Matt pressed the spikes into the sand around the two deck chairs. I had my towel laid flat out on the sand to sit on. I had spent some time paddling in the sea, then digging sand and building sand castles with my bucket and spade, uncle Matt bought for me on our walk to the beach this morning. I was sat on my towel, looking around the beach, watching other families playing and enjoying the holidays. The wind had started to build and the sand was being blown up and around us. We set about packing the windbreak, deck chairs and putting our rubbish in the bin. I put my shorts and t-shirt over my swimming costume and picked up my bucket and spade. The sky was getting dark with clouds, "I said it would rain today," said Uncle Matt. "Yes love, at least we managed to have our picnic before the wind got up. Let's hurry up back before the rain follows", said Auntie Lucy. We set off walking back along the same path we had walked earlier. I was sitting on my bed in our caravan, I had come in to find my socks and shoes for our walk later but I had fallen asleep on the bed. "Well, look who's awake. Sleeping Beauty. Did you find your socks and shoes?" said Uncle Matt. I nodded at him and got off the bed, picked up my socks and shoes and walked into the lounge area of the caravan. I sat down on the sofa. Auntie Lucy came to sit by me. "Uncle Matt had an idea whilst you were sleeping. As it's been raining and it's now stopped the sand and rocks will all be wet, an ideal time to catch crabs" she said. I looked up at her smiling and then over her shoulder to Uncle Matt who was walking back from the toilet. "Well, do you fancy seeing how many crabs we can catch? We can walk down the country path at the side of the camp site to the rock pools on the beach". I jumped up "Yes, yes, can we catch loads and then cook them and have crabs for tea like you have fish if you catch them?" I said. "We need to see if we can actually catch any before we make decision on what we will do with them" said Uncle Matt. I stood up and started to put on my white ankle socks. "No, no, not them one's love, they will get filthy, you need to put a pair of your coloured socks on and your pumps and your kagool". I run across the caravan to get my socks and pumps and promptly got ready. My kagool was a thin red waterproof coat with a hood. This would make me sweat if worn for a while. I didn't mind this though; I was so excited about going catching real live crabs. Auntie Lucy decided she would stay in the caravan and prepare our tea while Uncle Matt and I went to catch some crabs. I loved spending time with Uncle Matt, he was a nice and gentle man, very clever and knew the answer to all my questions and never told me to shut up. I would chat and chat for hours and he would indulge me and actually listen and respond to me. We had been down by the rock pools for a while now and we had both managed to catch a crab each. Uncle Matt showed me how you stand still and watch the crabs come up from under the wet sand between the rocks. We spent ages together, Uncle Matt would spend a lot of time taking photographs, he was a keen photographer and once we had caught our crabs, just before we set off back to the caravan for tea. I sat on the rocks, I had taken my kagool off now as the rain had stopped now and was drying up. I sat on some of the rocks and stared out to sea. I was sat daydreaming; unaware Uncle Matt was taking a photograph of me. I still look back at this photograph of a little girl in pumps, t-shirt and shorts with her hair in pig tails either side of my head and wonder if that little girl is now lost or is she still inside me? Something I will probably never know the answer to. Sadly, Uncle Matt is no longer with us, so I can't go to him to answer this question for me.

We got to the caravan with the bucket of crabs, uncle Matt had safely carried this back with us to show Auntie Lucy. I ran up the two steps to the caravan, flung open the door, "Auntie Lucy, come and see, we got some crabs, look, look", I said to her as I held her hand and escorted her to the door. Uncle Matt held up the bucket to show her. "Oh very clever, you can't bring them in here though, it would be cruel, the warmth of the caravan would make them feel too hot", she said. I let out a gasp, I was shocked she didn't want us to bring them in. What if someone pinches them whilst they are outside, I thought. "Don't worry, I'll put them under the caravan and put the net over them to stop them getting out or the campsite cats or dogs don't find them and eat them". I instantly relaxed, the cats and dogs won't be able to get to the crabs and I would be able to take them home and keep them as my pets, I thought.

We sat to eat tea together in the caravan then I helped to put away the dishes after Uncle Matt had washed and dried them. Once we had done this I was taken to the shower cubicles by Auntie Lucy. We went with our towels, soap and a bottle of shampoo. The showers were pretty quiet at this time of day so we were able to have showers next to each other and pass the soap and shampoo under the cubicles. Once back at the caravan I sat on the floor whilst Auntie Lucy brushed my wet hair and put my pigtails back in with red ribbons. We were all ready for our evening in the camp social club. We sat at a round table to the right of the stage, Uncle Matt had bought us drinks from the bar and we sat looking round the room. All of us looking in different directions watching other families. The music was loud and some children were up dancing on the stage and the dance floor in front of the stage. I sat daydreaming, I was enjoying every minute of my holiday, we had been here four days now and I had started to get to know some other children who were staying caravans. Julie came over to our table, "you coming over with us Edwina? Sarah said she is going to ask the DJ to play Shawoddywaddy's 'Under the Moon of Love' for us to dance to". I looked over at Uncle Matt for his approval, "Off you go love, stay in sight though and don't go outside the club". I walked towards the stage with Julie and started to dance to the music that was playing. Sarah and her little sister Tina came to join us. We carried on dancing and giggling to each other. Sarah was a small girl with red hair and had some blackness in her front teeth. She had a kind face and spoke with a different accent. She was from Wales and her accent was similar to many of the staff on the campsite and in some of the shops we went into. I liked Sarah, Julie and Tina, we swapped addresses and promised we would write to each other and become pen pals. I remember writing one letter when I got home from the holiday and received one letter back from Julie. No more contact after this though, I think we both just got on with our lives and left our holiday to memories. This could also probably be due to the fact I had lost the paper with the girls' addresses on. The following morning, I was up and about the caravan early, I was looking forward to going to help out at the stables and Auntie Lucy had bought some carrots yesterday so I could take them to the stables as a treat for the horses. I loved horses, despite having to clean out the stables using a large garden fork and brush and smelling of horse manure, I was loving every minute of spending time at the stables. I had a favourite horse, a light brown and white horse called Trigger, he was handsome and very calming and made you feel safe when riding him, even though he was a very tall horse. Once the stables had all been cleaned we set about brushing the horses then off we went to the kit room to get the horses saddled up for a ride. I could on just carry the saddle for Trigger, It was huge and very heavy, I picked this up after I had collected his bridle and hung this over my shoulder. I followed Karen's lead, mimicking her every move and feeling all grown up and like a true horse owner. I would pet the horses and talk to them just like Karen. She was a pretty girl, with short dark brown hair, big brown eyes and rosy cheeks. She was taller than me, a slim girl and always wore her riding jodhpurs and boots with a blue T-shirt that had the caravan site name and label across the back of it. She spoke with a very gentle sounding voice, her accent was different to mine, but not an accent I was able to put to an area. She was very welcoming and very pleasant, she showed me how to care for the horses, how to kit them up and helped me get onto Trigger before we went for a short ride along the outskirts of the camp site. Karen said this was advertising the riding school, showing all the children the horses and stopping half way around the site at the children's play area so the children could pet the horses and arrange to meet at the stables to book a riding lesson. I felt very proud riding round on Trigger whilst the other children watched us. Once back at the stables we unsaddled the horses and tethered them to the stable gates. It was now nearly 11.30am, I had been told my Aunt Lucy to make my way back to our caravan before 11.30. I picked up my coat and put it on. As I put my hand in the pocket and remembered the carrots and sugar lumps I had taken with me this morning. I walked around the stables and gave each of the five horses a carrot or sugar lump, petting each one as I walked away. I said goodbye to Karen and arranged to call back later in the day to help out settling the horses in stables for the night.

We walked around the small seaside town, looking in shop windows and walking into the odd shop to look around inside. I enjoyed our little shopping walks, holding Uncle Matt's hand and listening to him while he told me about the history of the little town. Last year he had come with Auntie Lucy and the shop on the corner had been a sweet shop that sold old sweets and toffee rock. Now it was a hair dressers salon. He told me the pub on the corner was a small, drab looking pub last year but now had been painted white and blue with an extended garden area with chairs and tables outside where people would sit enjoying a cold glass of beer. The little wool shop set in between the pub and the fish and chip shop, had been there for as many years as he could remember. He told me how he used to come for holidays here with his parents when he was a small boy and his mum would buy wool from the shop and make jumpers and cardigans for him and his brothers. I could walk around listening to Uncle Matt all day. He had a nice voice and was able to make everything he said sound interesting. We walked towards the chip shop and then uncle Matt decided we should buy a bag of chips and sit on the beach wall and eat them. We sat for about 30 minutes, eating chips, drinking fizzy pop and chatting. I was loving every minute of this holiday, no worries, no anxiety and it was now day four of our 7-day holiday and I had not had any accidents in bed. I could not explain or understand why this was, I never had an accident when sleeping in any bed other than my own. This caused frustration for me and anger from my mum and dad as they said I must be doing it on purpose if I could manage to stay dry at night in any other bed, then come home and wet the bed 8 out of 10 nights. We walked back to the camp site but walked up a steep hill by the side of the road, chatting and laughing as we walked. I skipped some of the way then I began to feel tired. "Come on little legs, keep going, not far now" said Uncle Matt who could see I was struggling to continue walking up the hill. Once back at our caravan I sat on the sofa with Uncle Matt playing cards. He was teaching me how to play a new game called gin rummy, I had only ever learnt how to play snap and fish. We must have been sat playing for ages, when I looked up from the table to Aunt Lucy who asked if we were hungry, I saw through the window behind her that it had gone dark and had started to rain. Uncle Matt and I both nodded, we were hungry and had been so engrossed in the cards we had not realised how much time had passed. That was one of the things about spending time with Uncle Matt and Aunt Lucy, the time always went so fast. Yet the time I was at home waiting for the weekend to come so I could go to stay over with them seemed to go on for ages. "Time flies when you're having fun", uncle Matt used to say and wink at me when I was looking sad and asking if I could stay a little longer when they were getting me ready to go back home on a Sunday evening after staying over with them.

We had eaten tea, I had helped Uncle Matt to do the dishes and we were now ready to walk over to the club house for the evening entertainment. Tonight was a cabaret act, Aunt Lucy said the lady in the campsite shop was telling her this act was not to be missed, everyone would be eager to go and watch this act. We were ready early, umbrella at the ready for Auntie Lucy and I had my own smaller umbrella, it was transparent apart from the edging being bright pink, it was like a dome shape and kept me dry despite the heavy rain. Once in the club house, Auntie Lucy held my hand and walked me to the table she wanted to sit at tonight, she wanted a good seat for tonight's entertainment. Uncle Matt went to the bar as we sat down around the table just off centre and behind just one table, the front row of tables was already full and the club house was a buzz of excitement, with music coming from the DJ and all the small children still enjoying the junior disco. I looked around for my friends for a few minutes but could not see them. "Edwina, sit down and sit still, you look like you have ants in your pants. We are early because I wanted to get a decent seat to watch the show tonight, I'm sure your friends will come in later". I sat back in my chair, still watching everyone who came into the door to see if any of my friends had arrived. Uncle Matt came to the table with a glass of wine, a pint of beer and a glass of juice, he was balancing the wine between the juice and beer. He had a packet of salted peanuts he was holding with his teeth. He put down the drinks and the peanuts. I watched as he put the wine in front of me, the beer in front of Auntie Lucy and he had the juice in front of him. "Bottoms up", he said and picked up the juice as if to drink it. "Hey that's my drink", I said. He looked down at the glass and then winked at me and said "oh eck, you're right, He then put the juice in front of me and then took the wine for himself and again he picked up the glass as to take a drink. I was giggling now, he always got things mixed up. "That's not yours, that's Auntie Lucy's". "Oh, so it is", he said looking down at the wine glass in his hand. "Heyyyy, what are you doing with my drink?" he said to Auntie Lucy. "Oh behave yourself Matt", said Auntie Lucy. He swapped the glasses, winked at me and then said, "Right young lady, am I allowed to drink this drink or does this one belong to anyone else"? I nodded still giggling at him getting his drinks mixed up. No matter how many times he would do this, I would always find it amusing.

The cabaret act was good, they sang some songs played the piano and guitar, told some jokes and even did a magic trick. I think everyone in the room was sat quiet watching this act. Once the act had finished the club began to start emptying of people and we got up and walked back to our caravan. The rain had stopped but it was very windy and cold. Once back in the caravan I got washed and changed and settled to bed. Tomorrow was our last day of our holiday so I didn't want today to end then tomorrow did not come too fast. I was loving the time we spent here. I could live in a caravan, I thought to myself. I would be able to spend time helping out with the stables and exercising the horses during the day or going to the beach and building sand castles or crab catching, then spending time enjoying the entertainment in the club house every night. Uncle Matt came in to my bedroom to say good night, as he always did. "Get a good night's sleep we have a long drive home in the morning. I bet you're missing your mum and Dad?" he said. I looked up at him and smiled, not knowing what to say. How could I be happy to be leaving my holiday behind? I was missing home at night times, it was very quiet in the caravan. No noise from the TV, no raised voices and no fighting or laughing coming from the boy's bedroom. I then started to think of all the things I would have to tell my friends when we go back to school. Uncle Matt kissed me on my head and stroked my hair from my face, "night night, don't let the bed bugs bite" he said as he walked towards the door and then switched off the light.

"Morning Eddy, make sure you get your wash bag ready before breakfast then we can walk over to the wash room before it gets busy then we can get the bags loaded and get on our way home and miss some of the traffic". I did as I was told and then walked to the lounge area to sit with Uncle Matt who was sitting drinking tea and eating toast. He was washed and dressed, back into his usual clothes, long sleeved shirt with cuff links and tie. His jacket to match his trousers laid neatly on the chair beside the dining table. It was definitely time to go home I thought. He had worn short sleeved shirts and on the warmest days he had even worn short trousers and sandals. Not today though, his shining black lace-up shoes were set beside the caravan door ready for when we left. I was still sleepy despite sleeping well and needing to be woken by Aunt Lucy this morning. The first time of the whole holiday, I had been first up and moving around making subtle noises to wake them, then our day's adventures and fun could start. "Well, well, you must be ready for going home if you're sleeping in love, I think this week of fun has taken it out of you", said Aunt Lucy. "Have you had a good time love?" said Uncle Matt. I looked up at him, nodding my head. I was feeling strange, a sense of loss and also a feeling of happiness and love for the two adults stood in-front of me. I was unable to speak, I don't know why, I just had a funny feeling in my throat that was preventing me from verbalising my feelings. As if he understood, Uncle Matt winked his eye at me and hugged me closer beside him. "I've had the best time but still don't understand how those crabs managed to get out of the bucket, we'll have to look out for them on our way home, we may see them trying to get to the beach at the zebra crossing". I started to giggle at the thought of this and my strange feeling started to subside. I had been upset when I realised the crabs had managed to escape from the secure place in the bucket under the caravan, thinking a cat or dog may have eaten them but Uncle Matt assured me this would not have happened. He explained how crabs need water to survive and their instincts would have been to get free and get back to the sea. He said we must have caught some very clever crabs who would have worked together to push off the net and escape when cats and dogs were all inside sleeping. This made me feel better that they had not come to any harm, but sad that I hadn't been able to keep them as pets. It was many years later when he told me he had actually taken the bucket for a walk back to the beach once I was in bed and sleeping.

I was staring out of the window watching all the shops we had visited in the past week. Driving along the coastline towards the town with my forehead leaning on the window when we went over a bump in the road, my head bobbed back and then into the window. I quickly leaned back and settled into the journey home.

Chapter Eight

The lunch time bell sounded, it could be heard along both corridors and into each of the class rooms. This was our signal to stop work and get up from our desks and make our way to the playground with our friends or to the canteen for lunch, depending on which lunch time sitting your class was allocated. Not in our classroom though, Mr Woods was one of the older teachers, strict and thorough. We soon realised once joining his class, that 'That bell is for my benefit and not yours, it merely reminds me that lunch time is approaching. So if you wish to partake in the lunchtime break then you must sit and participate in the class until I say the class has ceased and release you for your break.'

I loved spending time chatting in the playground with my friends, sharing our stories of our summer holidays. I felt a sense of pride telling my friends about my time at the beach, the ponies, the friends I had made and the escaping crabs. My best friend at school was called Sarah, she asked why I had gone on holiday with my aunt and uncle and not with my parents or siblings. I didn't have the answer, so I made up a story, telling them my dad was not being able to travel so soon after his serious accident. I explained that my aunt and uncle could only take one of us with them and as I had been so well behaved, they had chosen me, over my brothers or sister. I went on to tell them how I had been so upset about my dad that the adults in the family felt I was in more need of a holiday than my siblings. When in fact I had never asked any of these questions when my aunt and uncle arrived to take me on holiday, I just went along with the plan and didn't dare ask, for fear they would decide to take Lucy and not me. It didn't cross my mind that I was being untruthful, this was a part of my school life. Often I would tell stories of my home life to join in with conversations but most of the stories I would tell would actually be stories I had made up as I was talking. I couldn't tell them what really happened at home, I was too embarrassed. My friends would share stories of how they would be sat in bed and mum would come in to tuck them in or take them out for a treat and buy them something special. They would talk about the wonderful family holidays they had been on and how they had spent time in the holiday discos dancing with the children and adults would join in. I didn't have any stories like this to share, so I felt the only option was to make up my own stories. I was enjoying the interest my friends showed in my holiday. We were laughing, sharing our tales, each one impressing the group even more with every tale we told. The lunchtime bell rang out to signal that playtime was over, we all made our way back into school, filled with pride and happiness with our shared memories. I loved being in school with my friends, escaping to the routine of lessons, teachers, the same kids getting into trouble, reading stories as a class, being transported away into the books by the teacher's ability to use changed voices and use punctuation to express the voices and feelings of the characters in the stories. I enjoyed every part of the school day, even lunch time, being watched in the canteen by the dinner ladies monitoring what we had eaten then sending us back to finish our meal, whether we liked it or not. Wednesdays were the days I dreaded in the canteen, liver and onion or steak and kidney stew for main with chocolate sponge cake and green custard. I gagged at the meat every time and tried many different ways of not having to eat it. From refusing it at the hatch, only to be told I must try just a little as no other option was available. I would move the food around my plate, ask all the children on my table and surrounding tables if they wanted my meat. I had dropped the plate when taking my lunch tray to the cleaning area, monitored by another dinner lady. Only to be caught out after doing this for the 3rd week in a row. Mrs Hughes the dinner lady on guard/clearing duty would send me back up to the hatch to get a fresh main meal and she would sit me next to her for the remainder of the lunch break and watch me gagged and even vomit when putting the meat near my mouth. She would threaten to speak to mum and dad about my bad behaviour and refusal to eat. "Do you really think your mum and dad want you going home starving when you have a perfectly good meal to eat? No, they wouldn't," she would answer her own question and then back to the table I would go until either I had vomited or lunch break had finished and I was sent to stand outside the Head Teacher's office for bad behaviour then being scolded by the Head Teacher, Mrs Kensington who would say how shocked she was that I was again outside her office for this ridiculous refusal to eat. No matter how many times this situation played out, the outcome was always the same. I would get told off three times and then on the fourth occasion they would call my mum into school to discuss my behaviour. Mum would not be happy about this, I would be given a note by the Head Teacher to give to my mum. Every time I knew the outcome, she would refuse to come to talk to my Head Teacher, I would be in trouble at home for causing problems and refused pudding at tea time at home until she forgot about the school letter.

My school was a very small community school, in a small northern town, where everyone knew each other, all siblings either went to the school with you but in different classes or they had been to the small school before moving up the next stage of education. The daily routine only changed with the seasons, however despite the seasons mornings would always follow the same pattern where we would spend the mornings in assembly, listening to the head teacher talking about achievements, saying prayers and singing hymns. I would sit in a line on the floor with arms folded and legs crossed. Sitting with all my friends each playing with one of the others hair, putting plaits in or just twirling it to curl it.

Chapter Nine

Christmas was getting close, my younger brothers had all spent time looking in the boy's section of mum's catalogue and choosing what they wanted from Father Christmas. My sister had already written her list; she didn't need to look in a catalogue, she knew exactly what she wanted. I was undecided, I was waiting for my turn to look through the catalogue. I knew I wanted my own horse more than anything, but also knew we would never be able to afford a horse. The boys would end up falling out and mum would take the catalogue away and tell me I would get my turn tomorrow. I eventually wrote my list and put on all the things I thought we could afford. I listed a new pair of blue running pumps, my own hairbrush set, makeup and a game of frustration. One of my friends had brought the game into school to play on a rainy day when we were able to play our games during indoor playtime and we had a great time playing this. I asked for the game 'Operation', the buzzing noise and red nose light that went off if you touched the sides when removing bones from the patient looked great on the TV.

We all went to bed early, hoping we would get to sleep quickly, so morning time would come sooner. No matter how many years we tried this it never seemed to work. We were so excited we could not settle to sleep and mum would shout up a few times and then come upstairs when the noise level increased and warn us that Father Christmas will not come to noisy children who are not asleep.

When the morning came, it was still dark but the boys were up and in mum and dad's bedroom waking them up screeching with excitement and anticipation, wondering if they had been good enough for Father Christmas to stop at our house and bring us presents. We would all have to wait at the top of the stairs until mum had gone to switch on the lights. We ran down the stairs in a group, eager to be the first to see if he had been to our house. Dad would usually stay in bed whilst we opened our presents and then get up and join us down stairs when mum started to cook breakfast. When dad did come down we would all fight for his attention to be able to show him how good we had been because Father Christmas had brought our requested presents and also some surprises. This year one of my surprises was a gift from Aunt Lucy and Uncle Matt, a book called 'Little Women'.

Chapter Ten

Sunday nights, most weeks mum would get the girl from around the corner to come and babysit us all whilst mum and dad went out to meet friends in a pub. Dad would say this is play time for mums and dads and so we needed to be very good for the babysitter or when he came home we would all be in big trouble. We were able to sit and watch TV with the babysitter before being sent to bed at an agreed time, earlier if we were not behaving properly. Lucy was able to stay up longer than us younger ones, as she had kicked up a fuss earlier when dad was telling us the rules for the night. She was shouting and refusing to go to bed at 8pm as she stated that she was not a baby and didn't think it was a very good idea to go out and leave us all at home to go to a party, leaving us with the babysitter who was only three years older than her. She knew if she put up enough of an argument then dad would agree with her and she would be able to stay up for longer. She was sitting on the edge of the sofa, arms folded in front of her chest, refusing eye contact with dad who was trying to get her to smile. Lucy would always pretend she had fallen out with him, she knew this worked as it had never failed her in the past. She sat head held up looking out of the lounge room window, as if close to tears, sniffing now and then for effect if she thought he was losing interest. I knew she would get her own way, as I think mum and dad knew also. Mum had told her to just be quiet and stop acting like a spoilt brat. Lucy then gasped as if offended and looked to dad, her eyes filling with tears, again she knew this would get his full attention. "Right shut up now, leave her alone". It was working and Lucy knew it, I glanced over to her again and saw her slightly smile over to mum who was now looking angry and ready to reply to dad but thought better of it. Mum then walked out of the lounge muttering under her breath, I couldn't catch what she was saying. "Eddie, go make me a brew", he said. I stood up and walked towards the door, turning as I got to the door, he got up and walked up from the chair and walked over to Lucy, "What?" he said to me. "Tea or coffee?" I quickly asked. "Tea", he replied. As I left the room, closing the door I heard him "Oh come on now, ignore your mum, you can stay up, just don't tell the little ones, or they will all want to stop up". I knew it, yet again her manipulation had worked. She always got her own way, she just knew if she sulked and made enough of a fuss he would give in.

I had gone up to bed at the same time as the boys, when told. The boys were all racing upstairs, pushing past each other to get to the top first after the baby sitter had said, "last one to the top of the stairs is a smelly sock". As I eventually got to the top of the stairs the boys were singing "Smelly sock, smelly sock, Eddie is a smelly sock". "Shut it, all of you, go to bed and stop shouting". "Smelly sock, smelly sock", they continued. Once I had changed and got my night dress on, I walked across the landing to the bathroom. The babysitter had gone back downstairs after making sure the boys were all in bed. The house had gone quiet, only the dull sound of the TV could be heard at the top of the stairs. I got into the bathroom and sat on the toilet. The door burst open, all three boys giggling and squeezing in through the door, shouting, "smelly sock, smelly sock, Eddie is a smelly sock". I was startled and screamed at the shock causing the boys to laugh even more and even louder. I hadn't heard Lucy climbing the stairs, I only heard her voice when I saw Luke swiftly moved back from the door. Lucy had grabbed the back of his pyjamas and pulled him out of the door. "What the bloody hell is going on in here? Why are you not in bed? You always have to mess about at bed time. Well not tonight, you three get back in bed now". The boys were stifling the giggles and shuffling past Lucy to get back to the bedroom. I was still sitting on the toilet holding onto my night dress, trying to cover my modesty. Lucy stepped into the bathroom and slapped me across the face. I almost lost my balance and held onto the wall to keep myself sitting on the toilet. I could not retaliate and as I was not aware the slap was coming I had no time to defend myself. My cheek started to heat up from the slap. I instantly started to cry and shouted, "What was that for?" Lucy now stood over me, staring into my face, so close I could feel her breath on my face. "That is for winding them up and still pissing about. It doesn't take this long to get ready for bed. Now get to bed pissy arse and don't get up again or you will get what's coming to you, do you hear me?" I was now stood facing her. I walked towards the bedroom and as I reached the door, looking back at Lucy who was just about to go back down stairs. I was speaking my thoughts in a low tone, "Who does she think she is? She is not my mother, she can't tell me what to do, wait until I tell mum she slapped me, she's not getting away with that. One day". "One day what? What are you going to do?" Shouted Lucy. I walked into the bedroom slamming the door behind me. I got to the bed, just pulling the covers back, when the bedroom door opened. Lucy came rushing in, grabbed my hair and slapped my face again, then she pushed me onto the bed. Shouting "Yeah, like I thought, you won't do anything, now get into bed and think twice next time before answering me back". I was cowering on the bed now, crying, my head hurt and my face was smarting from the slaps. Lucy left the room and I wriggled under the covers, still crying. I must have drifted off to sleep whilst crying.

I woke up to the sound of raised voices and realised it was mum and dad, who had returned from the pub. Laughing and joking together. I was just about to turn over in my bed when I realised I had wet the bed. I wriggled to the side of the bed nearest the wall away from the wet area. I didn't dare get out of bed to get changed. It was dark and I couldn't visualise if Lucy was in her bed or not. I must have drifted back off.

"Quick, quick, come on love, get out of bed, Shhhhh, its ok, I just need you to come with me" It was Beryl, one of our neighbours. Was I still dreaming? Why would Beryl be in my bedroom? Then I heard his angry loud voice. I could hear other deep male voices too. The urgency in Beryl's voice was alarming, I started to cry, I was confused and scared. What was happening? Had he hurt her again? Who was he arguing with? Beryl was tugging on my nighty, trying to get me out of bed. Beryl then noticed my night dress was wet. "Oh, love, come on, its ok, we can sort this out, don't be scared, you can come to my house and we can get you warm". I felt embarrassed, scared and still very sleepy. Beryl knew I had wet my bed. I began to cry even louder, my cries reaching a pitch to match the noise of the men downstairs arguing. The shouting downstairs started to sound forced, they were getting out of breath. What was happening? I was intrigued as to what was happening downstairs but frightened as to what I might see when I finally got downstairs. Beryl had pulled a blanket off my bed and wrapped me in it. I walked slowly with her down the stairs to the open front door. A strange smell was getting stronger and stronger as we got to the closer to the open door. I first noticed a female police officer standing on the grass to the right of the garden path, she stepped forward towards me as Beryl walked behind me the female officer introduced herself as Sally, "it's ok sweetheart, come this way, pay no mind to them, everything will be alright, we are just going for a walk up to Beryl's house, get a nice cup of hot cocoa and have a sleep over. Would you like that? Come on your brothers are all at Beryl's too". I was trying to listen to the female officer but the noise from the male officers who were all in a heap on the grass on the other side of the garden path. I could hear a familiar voice shouting but I couldn't see him. Beryl stood to my left and the female officer stood to my right, blocking my line of vision from the male officers." Where's dad?" I asked. "Come on love let's get you out of the cold", said Beryl. The noise from the men on the ground got louder, one-man shouting "Just calm down. Get his legs, control him", said the man. What was happening, I wondered, my heart racing in my chest, I was scared and confused. Then I heard him, muffled and breathy, but angry, swearing and cursing. Saying what he was going to do to when he gets them one by one. I started to hold back the tears. Do they not realise what they were doing? They were in big trouble now, he meant what he was saying, I could tell.

Once I was at Beryl's, she took me to the bathroom, ran the bath and put in sweet smelling bubbles. I stood behind her in the bathroom. Beryl told me to take off the wet clothes then I could get into the bath. I stood behind her, feeling cold and scared, I could not get the picture of the officers fighting or the sound of dad and how angry he was. I didn't want to take off my clothes, my face was burning and I felt a strange feeling of embarrassment. Beryl was telling me she was going to make me and my brothers and sister a nice hot drink of chocolate. I could hear her talking but couldn't concentrate on what she was saying. I felt my eyes burning along with my face. Tears building up in my eyes. I was trying so hard to stop the tears but failed, I could feel the first tear touch my cheek, followed by a stream of tears. I sniffed up and tried to wipe the tears from my face, shaking my head from side to side to prevent further tears. Beryl turned around to see me stood shivering in my damp night dress, the blanket covering my shoulders. I could not stop the tears. "Oh my love, there, it's ok now, we are just going to have a sleep over. I know it's a shock to be woken from your sleep but we can have fun". Beryl stepped closer to me, put her arms around my shoulders and gently pulled me closer to her. My face resting in her tummy as she comforted me, rubbing my back and talking to me. I could not stop the tears, I could feel the pain in my chest and then in my throat, a physical pain, straining my throat, causing me to sob uncontrollably. I don't know how long we had been stood in the bathroom, me crying and Beryl soothing me. Beryl eventually stepped back and knelt down so her face was directly opposite mine, she held my chin with her index finger and stroked the back of my head, "now, now, come on, your ruining that beautiful face. Show me a smile, show me your beautiful little pearly whites". I started to calm down and forced myself to stop crying. I could not control the sniffling and sobbing but I was starting to feel even more tired. Beryl turned off the taps and asked if I would like to have a nice bath to warm me back up. She never mentioned that I had wet my bed, she stood up and then reached for a towel out of a cupboard underneath the sink. "Look, I have a nice fluffy towel for you, it's one of my favourites, it keeps you lovely and cosy after having a bath. I will get you one of Andrea's night dresses to change into because I think we got yours dirty on our way over here". I forced a smile and started to take off the blanket. I was a little embarrassed getting undressed in front of Beryl. At that point Beryl put her hand in the bath and tested the water, shook her hand and wiped it on the towel she had got out for me. "Ok the water is lovely and warm. You get into the bath and I will go get you a night dress. Once she left the bathroom, I quickly got myself undressed and stepped into the nice warm bath filled with bubbles. I relaxed back in the bath, pulling the bubbles over my tummy to protect my modesty in case Beryl came back in. Beryl came back a few minutes later, she tapped on the bathroom door, "It's only me sweetheart, I have the night dress here for you and a pair of socks to keep your feet warm". Beryl came into the bathroom, placed them on the floor near to the sink and then left. "You take your time and I will go get that hot chocolate".

Chapter Eleven

I rubbed my eyes and then focused, I quickly realised I was not in my own bed. I could feel my leg touching something. I turned over to see my brother lay at the bottom of the bed. We were at Beryl's house in Andrea's bed. I had been told to get into the bottom of the bed after my bath and hot chocolate as I had started to nod off whilst sitting in the lounge with Beryl and Lucy. Beryl had asked Lucy and me to share the sofa but Lucy had refused to lay next to me. So Beryl had crept up into Andrea's room and guided me into the bottom of the bed. I had gone straight off to sleep. Now, I lay for a few minutes, thinking about the events of the night before. I started to visualise the scene in the garden, the shouting and the threats dad was making and wondering what had happened. Had he hurt anyone? Was he in trouble and why had we been woken up and taken from the house? It wasn't the first time the police had been round to the house after a Sunday night out when neighbours had phoned the police due to the noise of mum and dad arguing and fighting but never had we been woken and moved to another house.

I could hear voices downstairs, I strained to hear the voices, trying to make out who was talking. I recognised a voice but could not work out who it was. I could not work out what they were saying. I gently slipped out of the bed, making sure I didn't make any nose or disturb Peter. I crept towards the bedroom door and gently opened it up slowly. I started to tip to across the landing to the bathroom. Beryl lived in a house exactly the same as ours so the bathroom was across the landing above the kitchen. i could hear the voices more now. "I think the gas man came about four and made it safe", said one voice. "How long before they can go back in?" said a male voice. "I'm not sure, they will have to make sure they get the all-clear from the police first. He totally lost it this time. It took six of them to get him in the van, one police man ended up with a bust nose". "Really? Oh he would have paid for that down the station, they don't like to see one of their own hurt. He will get what's coming to him. I don't care how big and strong he is, he isn't above the law, no matter who his mates are. Even his police mates won't be able to get him out of this one". I was stood at the top of the stairs when the voices seemed to get louder. I tiptoed away from the top of the stairs where I had stood listening to them talking. The kitchen door opened and Beryl walked from the kitchen, across the bottom of the stairs and I could hear the lounge door open. The floor boards at the top of the stairs creaked. I quickly tiptoed into the bathroom and closed the door as quickly and quietly as I could, closing the bathroom door. I stood behind the bathroom door, my heart racing, frightened I would be in trouble for 'ear wigging', as my mum called eavesdropping.

Beryl came upstairs and stood outside the bathroom door. She tapped gently on the door, "Eddy, is that you?" she said. I stepped closer to the door and opened it, "I, I, I was having a wee", I said in a nervous voice. Beryl lifted her hand to touch my shoulder, I cowered away. "Hey come on love, It's only me, I'm not going to hurt you, come on let's get you downstairs and get you some breakfast", she said, whilst tapping my shoulder and pulling me into her hip to cuddle me.

Beryl gently tapped me in the middle of my back, pushing me into the front room where mum was sitting smoking a cigarette in one hand and holding a cup of tea in the other. She looked tired with black eye makeup smudged under her eyes, wearing her new blue top and skirt. The clothes she had been wearing when she left to go to meet friends in the pub with dad last night. She looked up at me, "I might have known, you'd be the first up. Scared of missing something, are you?" she said, then looked back to her cigarette, put it into her mouth and sucked in her cheeks for what seemed like ten minutes but was probably less than one minute. Blowing out the smoke loudly, she looked back at me. "Oh for god's sake, sit down will you?" I quickly did as I was told and sat on the chair nearest the door. "Not there, on the floor, Beryl is sitting there". I quickly jumped of the chair, as if I'd just sat on a sharp pin and moved quickly to sit on the carpet in front of the fire. I had just sat down and crossed my legs in front of me, when Beryl came into the lounge with a dish of Weetabix with milk and sugar on it. "Here you go love, come sit on the chair while you eat your breakfast, you must be hungry", she said. "She can eat it on the floor, we're not proud" Mum said with an angry tone. I stayed sitting quietly on the floor and ate the Weetabix, making sure I didn't give mum any eye contact. She was angry and best not to bother her when she is in this kind of mood, I thought. The milk on the Weetabix was warm and Beryl had put lots of sugar on top, it was lovely. Just as I was finished eating, making sure I ate every last bit, mum snapped again. "Do you have to eat like a pig? What's wrong with you? You trying to piss me off? Because I can tell you, today is not the day. Why you have to be up at this time I don't know. Oh wait don't tell me you've pissed in Beryl's bed? Well, I can tell you now. That, is the last thing I need to hear. I don't have money to be replacing beds because you're too bone idle to get up and use the toilet like normal folk" she snarled. "Oh, come on, it's not the child's fault this has happened, she's had a disturbed night, go easy" said Beryl as she was bending down taking the bowl from me. "It can't be easy trying to sleep in a strange bed is one thing, being woken from your bed and walked around the street to a neighbour's house and sleeping in a strange bed is another. And no she hasn't wet the bed, she's just woken up early, that's all, isn't it Eddy?" I didn't reply or even look in mum's direction, I didn't dare. I sat staring at the carpet whilst mum was talking about the events of the previous night and how we had all ended up here. She was cursing and swearing, calling dad names continuously. This was nothing new to my ears, I had heard this many, many times before. Today she was concerned about having to clean up the mess and how much this was going to cost. She was cursing the police officers and the man from the gas board. "Why he couldn't just fix it and be done, save us all this trouble. Dragging my kids out of bed at that ungodly hour. Bloody good for nothing, that's what they are. They don't do anything useful but still expect the bills to get paid. If I wasn't on a meter, I would be seriously thinking about not paying the bloody bill. I can tell you". She went on and on about the gas man, police men and how she had been treated. I drifted into a daydream, thinking about the visions I had seen the night before. The face I woke to, the gentle voice and the fear I felt seeing the men all on the floor, shouting, the blue lights flashing on the police cars lighting up the street.

I had been sat daydreaming for quite some time before I stood and asked Beryl if I could use her toilet. Beryl winked at me and nodded to me. Mum had stopped cursing and was sat lighting another cigarette, sucking in her cheeks to light the end, then winced as the smoke went into her eye, then in snappy tone said, "Oh you bleeder" as her eyes stung. I quickly moved towards the door, aware my presence was irritating her. As I got to the bottom of the stairs and looked up I saw the boys were all stood at the top looking lost. "Eddy", said Luke, "Where's mum? Where's dad? Did you sleep downstairs? Did the coppers search our house? What's happened? Did everyone have to move house? Where did Davie and Jenny go? Are they here too?" I walked slowly upstairs as the quick fire questions were whispered in urgency. "What are you talking about? What would they be searching our house for? No one moved house, just us. We were moved for our safety because the man from the gas board couldn't be bothered to fix the gas. Mums downstairs with Beryl". I answered. Before I had finished the sentence all three of my brothers ran down the stairs pushing past me and into the lounge shouting the same questions at mum and Beryl. I heard mum shouting, "Right shut up the lot of you, let me think. Have you all forgotten your manners, say morning to Beryl and sit your backsides down and keep it down, for Christ sake".

A couple of hours later, I was walking back round to our house with mum, Lucy and Beryl. I was behind them trying to keep up with the fast walking pace. Mum and Beryl talking in code at what I guessed was the events of the previous night. The boys were told to stay watching cartoons with Peter, Beryl's husband. Peter was a very round short man, with grey hair and a very red large nose. He was a funny man, lots of fun and always smiling or laughing. The boys had been chatting away with him whilst watching cartoons in the front room and when given the choice of coming with us to clean up the mess from last night, or staying with Peter they opted for the latter.

Beryl asked mum what the police officer had said to her when he called before. Mum said he just said, it should be ok now to return to the house as the gas board had been round and said it was no longer out of bounds. "Did they ask Mr & Mrs Branner to move out last night? Mum just nodded, then said, "You can bet your bottom dollar she will be round giving it out later. Well I can tell you for one, I am ready for her today, if she dares say one word, so help me I won't be responsible". "Oh I don't think she will come round. Do you know where they went last night then? Do you think they went round to Kath's? I can't see them travelling down to

Ashton at that time of night to Kens, can you?" asked Beryl. "I don't have a bleeding clue, nor do I care. All I know is, if she dares to bother me with her petty gossip, or her holier than thou attitude, I won't be held responsible for my actions. I've had all I can take for one week; I can tell you. I've had it up to here" said mum, holding her hand in a salute like manner to her forehead.

As we reached the front door, I could feel my stomach churning and my heart beating out of my chest. I can't tell you why I was feeling so nervous, or what I was thinking I might see on the other side of the door. Mum put the key into the door and stepped inside, followed by Lucy. Beryl stepped aside and put her hand on my shoulder, smiling at me, "Come on Eddy, let's get this over with". I stepped into the hall and followed Lucy into the kitchen. We had a large wooden table with benches either side of it, where we would all sit to eat our meals. The table was pushed towards the wall and one bench was pushed into it but the other bench from the other side was nowhere to be seen. The cooker was in the middle of the kitchen floor. Not fitted between the cupboards like normal. The floor was a grey coloured lino, with mud and black scuffs all over it. In the sink was a smashed plate with parts of a dried up meal from yesterday's tea on every broken piece. Mum often made too much to eat and would plate up a meal for dad to eat later when he returned from the pub, or plate up his meal if he hadn't been home in time for tea. She would keep the oven on a low light to keep the meal warm for when he did eventually get home. The house had a strange odour, not a smell I could recall. It wasn't a nice smell, it was a dull and heavy smell. As I looked round the room I noticed Lucy and Beryl had both pulled their cardigan sleeves over their hands and covered their nose and mouth. I could completely understand why. "What is that smell?" I asked. No-one answered me, so I asked again. Mum was opening the windows and walking towards the back door to open it up. "What's with all the questions? Who do you think you are? Inspector Cluso? Just put a lid on it and start tidying up" she snapped.

I put my hand on the light switch as the only light was coming from the small kitchen window, it looked like rain outside so the dark clouds were making the room look darker than normal. "NOOOOOOOOO", mum shouted. I jumped back quickly, stumbling over myself with the shock and slipping and falling backwards into Beryl, standing on her foot. "For Christ sake, child, just leave things be will you? How many times do you need telling, you're not to touch anything? And I mean anything, OK?" I stepped to one-side of Beryl conscious I may have injured her foot and stood with my back to the sink, fear tearing through my whole body. What had happened to our kitchen? Why was I not allowed to switch on the light? I was helping, or so I thought.

"Can you believe it? The state of this place, all because the bleeding gravy had dried up. I mean, what did he expect after six hours in the oven? I won't be saving his tea again and that's a dead cert, he can piss off to the chippy in future, or starve, either way I don't care less. I'm not putting up with this".

Beryl now stood reassuring me with her arm around my shoulder, holding me to her for comfort. Lucy was stood in the doorway, none of us speaking, just looking on, in disbelief at what he had done. We all stood quiet, listening to her, as she walked around the kitchen passing the cooker to get to the other side of the kitchen. "Did you say the police had been given the all clear for you to return to the house with the children?" Beryl asked mum. "Yeah, a fat lot of use they are, keep you out of your house all night, arrest your husband and refuse to give you a lift to go see him at the police station when they are going to the exact same place. Bastards, the lot of them". Beryl reached round my shoulders and put her hands over both my ears to protect me from the abusive language my mum was using. I knew she was angry now, even more than usual. Mum was always swearing, saying bloody, bleeder, bleeding and swine when shouting at us. But never did she say words like bastard or stronger words unless she thought we could not hear when fighting with dad when we were in bed or in situations like this. "Oh don't worry about her, she's as thick as two short planks, she probably thinks all this is fun. Thinks it'd be clever to switch the light on and blow us all to kingdom come. I tell you I don't know where I went wrong with that one". Mum said. I could feel my heart pounding in my chest, a lump in my throat and a strong need to go to the toilet. I held back the tears that were stinging my eye lids. Beryl held me closer to her, trying to give me a reassuring hug. This made me feel even more emotional, I wasn't used to so much affection.

Only granny hugged me or kissed me I thought to myself. I looked to the floor at the black pumps I was wearing. Beryl had found them for me to walk from her house to ours. I started to move my foot around the floor, marking out two U's in the dust in the floor. I wasn't sure where all the dust had come from.

Lucy walked from the kitchen door towards the cooker, bent down to the over door and opened it. "Nowt in there now, does this mean the cooker is broken? Do we need to get a new one?" Lucy asked mum. "How the bleeding hell do I know? You can ask your father when he gets home, if they ever let him out, that is. That bleeding female sergeant would not tell me anything last night. She just kept parroting on and on". Mum then flipped her hair over her shoulder, put her hand on her hips in a mocking fashion, "Well assaulting a police officer is a serious offence, not to mention endangering lives. Plus, YOUR husband is not the only prisoner to be arrested tonight. He will be released sometime in the morning, that is IF, they decide to let him go to await his court hearing", she said in a very high pitched well spoken mimicking tone. She was red faced and picked up a cup from the kitchen side and threw it over towards the sink just missing Beryl and I. The cup had smashed in the sink, resting on top of the broken plate. Beryl and I jumped to the side. "NOW, that's enough, you just missed Eddy, I know this is difficult for you but getting yourself all upset and angry isn't getting this house back in order, is it? If you think about it, they would not have told you, they had the all clear for you to return if the risk of explosion was still apparent, would they?" Mum stood as if registering the information from Beryl, "I suppose you're right, sorry love, I'm just angry, you know I don't mean any of it" she said to Beryl. Lucy then picked up a side plate from the floor and followed mum's lead and threw it into the sink. The side plate also smashed. "Oi, what the hell are you doing? Give over, we'll have nothing left at this rate" Mum said. "It was cracked, not as if I caused this, is it? Maybe instead of keep shouting the odds, you should start to clean up. You know dad will be fuming if he comes home to this".

Mums face turned scarlet red, she inhaled for what seemed like an age, "HE will be fuming, Him? Listen to yourself will you, he bloody caused this. Pissed up and more interested in his stomach than his kids' lives, the stupid swine. And you best keep your trap shut girl, I'm in no mood to be listening to any shite that comes from your misguided loyalty, I can tell you. That saint of a man could have killed all of us last night with his bully boy antics, you included my dear, so don't come the holier than thou princess routine with me, because I can tell you it won't wash" she said. Walking past Beryl and I, mum then switched on the light with a heavy tap of the switch. She was even angrier now than I could ever remember. Shouting at Lucy, the look of anger on her face, was scary and not something often witnessed. Lucy generally stayed in mum and dad's good books and despite her princess behaviour, mum usually just ignored it. Not today though, she was in the firing line for mum's bad mood. I stepped back pushing my back into the kitchen sink to avoid getting in her way when she turned round to look back on the kitchen again. Lucy stood at the opposite side of the kitchen with an incredulous look on her face. She wasn't used to being spoken to like that and appeared to be struggling to keep her thoughts to herself. She mumbled something as mum stood looking at the kitchen. "WHAT WAS THAT? What have you got to say? Tell me? Go on, you normally don't keep your opinion to yourself, come on, say it, whatever it is, spit it out", said mum. Lucy put her head down, tears in her eyes, she walked towards the back of the kitchen, opened the back door and left, slamming the door behind her. Mum shouted after her, "Truth hurts don't it princess, well stick around long enough, I have lots of truths for you. Just think on, when you're blaming me for this, it's your darling daddy who caused this, no one else, him and him alone". She then went silent, stood for a minute or two then said, "Looks like you're right Beryl, the light switch didn't blow us up, so time to get this shit sorted out and clean up his mess". She said. "Eddy get the dustpan and brush, bin bags and bleach from under the sink, it's not going to get sorted with us stood looking at it". I did as asked and we set about cleaning the kitchen. Sweeping, mopping, and putting the table and bench back in the right place. Beryl had gone to the back garden to put a rubbish bin in the dustbin and shouted for me to come help her carry the other kitchen bench in. Once the table and benches were set straight, all three of us pushed the cooker towards it original home between the cupboards. The cooker was heavy and felt like it was stuck to the floor. Even three of us pushing at the same time didn't seem to move it very far. Once we had moved it a few inches, we stood back all panting for breath, Beryl was coughing continuously and gasping for breath. "Oh that'll have to do, I don't have it in me to push any more", said mum. "Am I glad to hear that? I felt like I was going to cough up a lung" said Beryl, still coughing. Mum and Beryl then stood back and lit a cigarette each, inhaled and then both sat on the kitchen bench to rest.

A few hours later it looked like nothing had happened, apart from the cooker still standing out of place but nearer to the cupboards than before.

We all stood by the door admiring our efforts, Beryl put her hand on my shoulder and squeezed. "Well, I for one think we've earned a cuppa, what do you think? You want a cuppa or a cold drink Eddy?" Beryl said. "Oh don't mind her, put the kettle on, make me and Beryl a brew", said mum. "Don't know what we're going to have, for tea. Nothing cooked, that's for sure, but at least we can have a brew", she said, walking with Beryl to go sit down in the lounge and wait for me to follow with the cups of tea.

Chapter Twelve

Whilst making them both a cup of tea my memories of the night before came back to me like a movie scene. A police officer had come to my bedroom and shook my shoulders, then, in a hushed voice, I was told to get out of bed and to put on my shoes and coat. The female officer held out my coat so I could put my arms into the sleeves, I wasn't thinking anything and didn't question anything. I just got out of bed and did as I was asked. I could feel a sense of urgency, not enough time to stop to get fully dressed. I was escorted down the stairs by the police officer and straight out of the house, into a waiting police car where mum was waiting in the back seat. She looked worried with a tear stained face of mascara under her eyes giving the clues she had been crying. A male police officer was sitting in the driver's seat. I was led to the other side of the rear of the car and asked to get in and put my seat belt on. Again I did as I was told and sat patiently as the male police officer, car drove away from our house. We drove for what seemed like an hour in silence. The noise of the beeping and some transmission or talking coming from the officer's radio's was the only sound to break this silence. The longer the journey, the more my thoughts would race around in my head. Was I in trouble? Was I being taken to prison? Where were we going? What had mum done wrong? Were we going to prison, together? Had she been crying because I was being taken to prison and she had been pleading with the officers not to take her baby girl away? The more I thought the more I could feel heat rising from my feet to my head. My heart pounding out of my chest. The silence was eventually broken by the female officer, "Are you alright love?" she asked me, turning her head towards the car door to look over her shoulder at me. At this point I realised I was breathing very heavy and panting for breath. I instantly looked up to meet her gaze and nodded my response. "Oh don't looked so worried, its ok, we are just going on a little trip, you will be fine once we get there. It must have been a shock me waking you up like that? Don't worry, your mummy will tell you all about it when we get there. You can have a nice warm drink and then get some sleep. Mummy will be with you all the time, no one will leave you on your own, so no need to look so worried". She said in her quiet yet squeaky voice. She was a pretty lady, with blonde hair in a ponytail at the back of her head. Very pale skin and beautiful blue eyes that looked like the sea. She winked at me before turning her head back round to face the front window. The male officer had been talking into his radio whilst she had been talking to me. He had told the person on the other side of the radio that we were on route and the ETA was approximately 12 minutes. It was morning now and I could feel my body shivering, I pulled the cover over my head without opening my eyes. Last night's events rushing through my mind, with vivid recall and colour. Every word echoing in my ears. Playing over like I was watching a movie. As I tucked my legs into my abdomen, my foot just touched mum's leg. I quickly moved to make sure I didn't wake her. I had woken last night as she got into bed. I was facing the wall so didn't move so she would think I was still sleeping. She was sniffling and wiping her nose. I could feel the bed clothes move as she moved. This went on for some time, before I realised she was crying. I could feel a pain in my stomach, a knot in my throat. I didn't dare move but felt like my heart was going to break with the pain and sadness this noise had conjured inside me. She must have cried herself to sleep. She was holding her face into the pillow to dampen the sound. She cried and cried, for what seemed like hours. The more she cried the more I felt the pain. I can't remember anything else from that night, I must have fallen to sleep. I lay in the bed, daydreaming about school and my friends. 'Will they be missing me? Will they wonder why I am not in school? Will they think I have been on holiday again? Would I ever see them again?' The answer to every question was unknown. Mum eventually turned over in bed to face me, "Eddy, are you awake?" She said in a low voice. I opened my eyes, to see her, both our heads on the pillow. We were in a small single bed with two covers to share. The room had a funny musty smell about it. Our bed was in the corner of a small room. I think it was an attic room, as I remembered walking up two flights of stairs then a smaller staircase with not as many steps. It was dark when we arrived during the night, despite the small bedside lamp on a small table by the head of the bed on the right side. The other side of the bed was against the wall with a very small set of curtains hung over what must be a very small window. I hadn't taken much notice of the décor last night. The journey to this house took us quite some time. Once alone in the bedroom, mum had said we're here as this was classed as a place of safety and that we would be looked after for a while until we could get our own house and then get my brothers and sister to live with us. She told me Lucy had woken and gone down into the lounge. Once the police were called they had spent some time chatting to mum who told them she needed to get away from him. They had offered to take her and all us children to this place of safety but Lucy had refused to leave dad and the boys had slept through all the shouting and fighting so mum had decided to leave them in bed as she had told the police officers he wouldn't hurt a hair on their heads. She told the female police officer she was worried about leaving me in his care as she said he would blame me and he had the potential to harm me, to get back at her. This was the only explanation I was ever given for the reason I was removed from my bed that night. It had started like most Sunday nights. We would stay up with the babysitter when mum and dad went out to the pub. Then we were all put to bed and once asleep, I was woken by raised voices that on some nights would subside and settle for a while. Then I would hear them both walking upstairs and into their bedroom. Not this Sunday night though, Lucy and I heard them come home and say goodbye to the babysitter, then within minute they were shouting at each other and before long they started to make banging and smashing noises. This lead to them actually fighting. He was threatening to slit her throat and shut her up for good. I don't know what started the argument but as always, Sunday night had turned into fall-out night. Returning from the pub angry with each other, the similar sounds would play out. I was sat in my bed listening to the argument increase in severity. I heard her scream and shout "Get off me. No, No don't". I don't know what he was doing to hurt her, I assumed he must have hit her again. This was not the first time he had hit her. They had been arguing and fighting for quite some time. They would move from the lounge which was situated underneath my bedroom, to the kitchen underneath the boy's bedroom and bathroom. I heard the kitchen drawer and all the cutlery rattle. My heart began beating faster and faster. Had he got a knife out to slit her throat? Oh NO, where is she now? I thought. Get Out, Get Out, I was saying over and over in my head, then I pulled the covers over my head. I didn't want to hear them shouting, I didn't want to hear him slit her throat. I quickly pulled the covers back off my head. Despite not wanting to hear them, I needed to listen. My instinct was to run. Get out of bed and try to get out of the house without him knowing. I mapped out my escape route in my head. I would crawl along the bedroom floor, onto the landing, wait until they had gone into either the lounge of front room and closed the door. I was then planning on creeping down the stairs as quietly as possible, out of the front door, creep under the kitchen window, then run as fast as my legs would take me, across the road to the side of the house to the nearest telephone box to call nine, nine, nine and get the police to stop him from killing her. I jumped at the sound of his heavy footsteps coming up the stairs. My body started to shake involuntarily,

I couldn't stop it. I needed to stop the shaking, he would know I was awake if he saw this. My heart racing faster and faster as he got closer to the top of the stairs. "Who the hell is that? at this time?" he said. I was still shaking under the covers. I started to wet myself. I squeezed my tummy muscles as tight as I could, putting my hands between my legs to hold onto my urine. NO, NO, I can't wet myself, he will smell it, I will get into more trouble. I couldn't stop it. "POLICE, OPEN THE DOOR PLEASE", said a very loud voice. I felt a small amount of wet touch my hand. "Oh for pity's sake, wake the whole bleeding street, why don't you? Ever heard of knocking like normal folk?" Dad said. With that I heard his footsteps start to descend the stairs. "What bleeding time do they call this? coming round bothering good folk, WHAT THE HELL DO YOU WANT?" he shouted back. I felt myself relax, they were here to save her, they knew he was going to kill her. "Good night to you sir, we've had a report of violence and noise, we are here to talk to you about the report, may we come in and talk to you?" said the male voice. "No you can piss off, you're not wanted round here, we've not heard any noise or reported any violence, why don't you get out there and do your job, arrest the real culprits and stop harassing good folk?". "That's as may be Sir, we have had a report of noise and we have a duty to respond. Now if we could just come in and discuss this then we can be on our way and let you get to bed?" I'd started to feel better once the police had arrived at our house. I could hear a female voice and another male voice, trying to reason with him and calm him down, with very little success. I could hear more male voices, speaking with him and advising him that making threats to life was not acceptable and the noise he was creating had caused a member of the public to contact the police. No matter what they were saying he continued to shout at mum and make threats to harm her and shut her up, once and for all. Once the noise calmed down, I took my opportunity to get to the bathroom and back again as fast as I could. Back in bed the noise had reduced. I could hear muffled sounds but was unable to make out what was being said. I eventually drifted back to sleep. Mum was still looking at me, she sighed and then got out of the small bed, I followed her lead, walking behind her down the staircase to the bathroom. Mum tapped my back and gave me a little push towards the toilet to signal to me to use it first. We both washed our hands and face then returned up to the bedroom. Mum opened a drawer in a small set of drawers at the bottom of the bed. She took out a pair of clean knickers and a vest for me. They fitted perfectly. Then she passed me a green skirt and blue blouse, she told me to try them on for size but both were too big for me. She then found a red T shirt, I tried this on too. This was a little too big but would do, said mum. The skirt was the only one in the drawer that was anything close to my size so she tucked in the T shirt then said we would ask if the people in the house had a safety pin to help hold the skirt in place. Until then I would need to hold on to the skirt to stop it falling down. She found a pair of black boy's ankle socks, handed them to me. I put on the socks and then my school shoes I had worn for the journey here last night. Mum put on her black pencil skirt she had worn last night, then found a yellow blouse for her in the next drawer down. The colour looked nice on her, but when she turned to face me her pale face with no makeup on and her red eyes did not seem to match the bright coloured blouse. She found a pair of tights in the drawer, sat on the edge of the bed rolling them up her legs then stood and wriggled herself into them. She put on her shoes and then made up the bed. I was still standing near to the bedroom door, watching her, when she looked over to me. "Right Eddy, you be polite, no asking questions and no asking for anything, if you are offered something then fine but do not be rude. These people have offered us a bed and somewhere safe to stay, so you have to behave or we will have nowhere to stay and end up homeless. He would love that". I nodded my agreement, then followed her down the three flights of stairs. I could smell bacon cooking, my favourite. I loved it when dad was in a good mood on Sundays, he would cook Sunday breakfast, eggs, bacon, black pudding, sausages and beans for all of use with several rounds of white sliced bread. We entered a small kitchen, with faded green wall paper on the walls, a free standing cooker with high level grill in between the cupboards to the left of the door. Several low level and high level cupboards in a dark wood with several handles missing. A small round table to the right of the door with five mismatched chairs around it, a baby's high chair at one end of the table. A small boy was sitting in the high chair eating Weetabix from a pink plastic bowl and a drinking juice from feeder cup in. The little boy looked over to us at the door and lifted his spoon to point at us, the Weetabix falling from the spoon onto the floor at the side of the table. A tall thin lady stood with her back to us at the cooker. She had very long dark hair tied high up in a bun on her head. She was wearing blue jeans, pink fluffy slippers and a pink skintight T-shirt. She turned to the door to face us. "Morning, I'm Sally, you must be Eddy and Della? Sit down, sit down, can I get you a tea? Coffee? Would you like a glass of vimto?" she said to me. "That would be lovely" said mum. "Come on Eddy don't be rude answer the kind lady". "Oh stop it, it's Sally, were all friends here, she can have whatever she wants", said Sally. "Yes please", I replied in a quiet voice. "Bacon butty?" Sally asked us. "No, no, we couldn't possibly take your food", said mum. "Oh behave, like I said we're all friends here, you aint got no one if you aint got friends, let me tell you. Take what you can, when you can, it's not on offer every day. Besides you can cook dinner and I won't be saying no", she said. "Well in that case, that would be lovely, thank you". "And for you my beauty? Would you like a butty too?" I looked up to mum for the answer. "Well? Answer the lady Eddy, cat got your tongue?" she snapped. "Yes please" I said. "Now that's more like it. Get your chops round that girls, set you up for the day that will" said Sally. I liked Sally, she had a kind face, a strange accent that I hadn't heard before but seemed nice, all the same. "Oh Tommy, look at you now. I told you we had visitors, I asked you to stay clean and not make a show of me, you mucky pup", said Sally in a loving voice to the little boy in the highchair, who just looked up at his mummy with love in his big blue eyes. Sally kissed his forehead before starting to clean him up. Tommy was happy with Weetabix all over his face, he cried and twisted his head away to stop Sally from cleaning him up with the face cloth. Once clean he stopped the crying as she lifted him out of the chair and sat him on her knee. Sally then started to talk with mum about the other residents in the house. I was playing peek a boo with Tommy, listening to him giggle a little more every time I moved my hands away from my face. I wasn't listening to Sally's run down of the other people who were resident in this house. Tommy then looked up and started to lift his hands up, gesturing to be picked up, I was just about to stand and ask if he could be put on the floor so I could play with him, when I realised someone was standing behind my chair. Smiling at Tommy, the lady from last night walked around the table towards him and lifted him up into her arms and gave him a kiss and then placed him on her hip as she walked towards the kitchen sink. She turned to face mum and I, "You sleep ok? Not the best room I know but you're safe here and that's what matters. We can sort out all your paperwork once you have had time to settle in. We will speak to the police about them escorting you when you return to your home to collect some of your belongings and then look into getting appointments with social security to get you some money, then talk with housing aid about getting you on the list for a flat or house. Will your other children be joining you?" She didn't pause for an answer, she just continued asking mum questions "Do you have any family that could help out with getting your clothes and meeting you somewhere with them, then you don't have to risk him returning whilst you are in the house? Then we need to sort young Eddy out with school. Depending on what they say at housing, if it's going to be some time then you might be better to get her into an emergency place at our local school, then transferring her when you are settled in your own place. They are nice at Our Lady school, they have taken a few of our children for short term placements from here, they work well with us and understand the challenges some of the children face. They don't judge like some schools" she said. I looked from her to mum, fear rising inside me. Change schools? I don't want to change schools, I like my school, I have my friends, I don't want any new friends. I won't know anyone, they won't know me, what if they don't like me? Mum started to cry, silent tears rolling down her face at speed. "Oh come on love, it's not as bad as it sounds, you've had a shock, I'm here to help, you won't have to do any of this alone. I'm just getting you ready for the next few days. If you are serious and you are definitely not going back, your future starts here and the sooner you start making plans to move on, the better you will feel and the sooner this will all happen. Mark my words you won't thank me now, but you will in time, won't she Sally? What's Ellen like now? Tell her". Sally just looked over at mum, sitting with a toilet roll in her hand, wiping her tears that continued to fall down her face. Sally stood up and walked over to mum, pulled a chair to face her and sat down, reached out her arms and hugged her. She sat holding her for a while, "Oh dear, it's the shock, the reality of it all! I know, I know, it's hard it's going to be one of the hardest journey you have ever had to take but we will help you, every step of the way. Today I think you should just get used to the changes and have some time to think before you set about making appointments. What I will say is, one day, you will look back on today and see that all is good and you no longer have to live in fear. Your children will feel happier and you will all blossom as a family. You've made the decision to leave him and I can tell you it's not the easiest decision to make so you're half way to the finish line already". Mum sat with her head in her hands, shoulders shaking, sobbing uncontrollably. I felt tears building behind my eye lids, a tightness in my throat as I held back the pain of wanting to cry with her. I sat staring at her for a few minutes, whilst Sally hugged her. After what seemed like an age, mum's tears stopped as she wiped her eyes and blew her nose on the toilet roll. "Ok, let's talk about this later when the children are in bed and you have had some time to get your head round it all" said the lady who had walked in. "Eddy, is it?" she asked me. I looked up to her and nodded my head, not able to speak for fear I would burst into tears and set mum off again. "Well look at those beautiful brown eyes, and that dazzling smile, don't look so worried, everything is going to be just fine. Now you're here in Bella's house we have lots of toys to play with, lots of films to watch. A video recorder for you to watch the movies on. You can think of this as a little holiday. I know you're probably missing your brothers and sister, but hopefully you will soon be together and back to normal. Mummy brought you here to keep you safe and to enjoy yourself. So tell me. What would you like to do today?" I sat looking at her listening to her, unable to decide what I wanted to do. I wasn't sure if I trusted her, I felt uneasy about her. She had come into the room and upset mum and then told me this was a holiday. Holidays were supposed to be fun. I wasn't having much fun. I was holding up my skirt, feeling scared but wasn't sure, what I was scared of. "Come on, let's take Tommy into the lounge and choose a video for you both to enjoy, take your mind off the adults for a while". She held out her hand to me and nodded to Sally to bring Tommy into the lounge. I stood up, still holding my skirt up in one hand and the other hand holding onto my glass of vimto. We walked into the lounge, a very small, cold room with old and used furniture. The curtains were missing hooks and the net curtains were a dull grey looking colour. The sofa was dark blue with stains on it, a grey cushion on one side and a blue cushion on the other side. An armchair beside the fire that had a multi-coloured knitted cover over it with a plum coloured cushion and another armchair to the opposite side of the fireplace with a stack of children's used books on it. A small portable TV on a table under the window with a VHS video recorder sitting on the floor under the table. Videos were stacked up either side of the recorder. The smell in the room was cold and damp, not inviting or pleasant. I stood in the doorway trying to hold back the tears, feelings of nausea rising in my throat. I couldn't hold back the tears or describe my feelings. I was hurting, a deep hurt inside me that I didn't understand. I was happy to be away from him, I'd wanted nothing more for as long as I could remember. I feared him but wanted so desperately for him to love me and show me the slightest amount of affection. A small amount of love not the amount he showed Lucy and the boys, just acknowledgement that I was part of the family and that he cared would have been enough for me. Why did he dislikes me so much? Why had I been taken to this awful place, not given a choice to stay at home with my own toys and videos? I know I would have opted to leave for the adventure. But I wasn't given the choice, I was woken by a stranger and taken from my warm bed to this cold and dirty house. Sharing a small single bed with mum in a small dirty room. Left here with the ladies I had met only a few hours previous. I didn't mind Jimmy, he was a baby and probably didn't have the choice to come to this house either. Bella shouted for my mum to come into the lounge. Sally put Tommy down on the chair with the books and came towards me, took the Vimto from my hand, passed this to Bella and hugged me to her. "Come on love, it's not too bad, you will soon get used to it, it's been a shock for you, it's all happened so fast. Come sit with me and tell me what's worrying you". We walked towards the sofa and sat down together. Bella turned on the TV and put in a video for us to watch and Tommy sat up, eyes glued to the TV. Mum didn't come into the lounge, so Bella said she was going to see if she was ok. I sat with Sally, unable to express my feelings or even speak. I sat beside her looking at the TV as if watching the video. The nausea was building in my throat, the tears still stinging the back of my eyes. What has my life come to? What is going to happen to us? Were we going to have to live in this smelly house with these strangers for long? Questions flooding my thoughts, exhausting me.

Chapter Thirteen

We had been here for over a week now, the house was still dirty and damp with a nauseous smell. Our bedroom was small but mum had taken the bedding to the local launderette to wash and dry them. She had found a small vase with some artificial flowers in one of the cupboards in the sideboard in the lounge and put them on top of the bedside drawers to brighten up the room. She was in a good mood today and had not cried herself to sleep for the last two nights. She had gone to the social services a few days ago to get some money sorted. She said they had sorted out an emergency fund for her so she could buy some food for us to keep in our cupboard and pay Sally back for the food she had shared with us. We had been allocated two cupboards in the kitchen to put our food in. Every family had the same number of cupboards. Mum had said we needed to be careful with the food and make it last as she didn't know when she would get more money. She had gone out shopping with Bella and I stayed at the house again with Sally. It was late afternoon and mum had said I was to have a bath and wash my hair before she came back from the shops. I was sick of being stuck in this house but mum had given the same response as every other time when I had asked her if I could go out with her to the social or the solicitors. "You won't enjoy it Eddy, standing in queues waiting in waiting rooms until someone is free to talk to you. Plus, you should be in school. Do you want me to get into trouble? You know the truancy board will be on my back if you get seen walking around town with me. I really don't need any more hassle. Don't you think I've got enough going on?" She always made me feel guilty for asking. Sally had offered to watch me again as she didn't have the cash to go anywhere. "They don't give you enough to buy food let alone clothes. How they expect you to dress your kids on the pittance they give you, is beyond me" Sally said at every possible opportunity. She had filled the bath for me, put in some of her nice sweet smelling, bath crystals and offered to dry my hair with her hair dryer. She put it up into a ponytail with a black ribbon to match my black skirt that she had picked out for me. I was getting used to the house but wanted to go outside. For the whole time we had been here, I hadn't been allowed to go out. They had told me I should stay inside until the police were sure dad had no information about where we were staying. Mum said if he saw me, he would snatch me and use me as bait to get her back. She had met with the police officers earlier in the week. They told her that he had been down at the station many times asking for our address as he felt he had a right to know where they had housed his wife and child. This didn't make me feel any better, I was feeling more like a prisoner than I did at home. Always having jobs around the house to do after school, but at least I got to go to school and get out of the house during the day. I wasn't able to go to school yet as the end of term was two weeks away and no schools were willing to take on more children this late in the school term, so I would have to wait until after the two-week school holidays. She had said I would be able to go to school and make new friends but only when the police were sure he would never find us. My life was different from my friends at school, I was the one peeling potatoes for the family for tea. Keeping mum and her friends topped up with tea and coffee and all the while other children enjoyed the sunshine, or rain for that matter, but spending time with each other after school. They didn't have jobs to do, they were told to get changed and go out to play whilst the mums would be getting tea ready for the family. I didn't feel any different from my friends, this was my life and I was used to doing my jobs. I was used to not being allowed out until my jobs were done, to find she would have another job for me to do if I did actually manage to complete the jobs she had initially set for me. I soon realised this and took my time with peeling the potatoes. Lucy was allowed out, the boys were sent to play out after they had changed out of school clothes. Not me... no I was stuck in the house nearly every evening to do my jobs. Now I was stuck here in this dirty house, in the middle of a town I had never seen before and still hadn't seen much of because she was scared he would take me. She was ok to go out though, I thought. Why would he want to take me? He wasn't interested in me, he was only interested in her. I ran up the two flights of stairs to our small attic room and slammed the door behind me. Panting for breath, as I reached the top, I opened the door with such vigour the door flew open and creaked loudly swinging back to shut itself with a loud bang. I ran into the room and threw myself onto the bed, crying for the freedom I had never known. I cried for so long, I had eventually forgotten why I was crying and fell to sleep on top of the bed, fully clothed.

Chapter Fourteen

I had eventually been allowed to walk with Bella to the shop on the corner of the street. This was the second time I had been to the shop in the past three days. I wasn't allowed to play in the garden of the house. None of the children were allowed outside the house alone. "I have to make sure all the ladies are safe in my care", said Bella." Children playing in the garden can give rise to suspicions and we cannot afford gossip about how many different families come to stay here? The community only accept us using this property as a refuge as long as this does not impact in a negative way on the community as a whole". I was warned several times before we left the front door of the house, I would have to hold tight to Bella's hand all the way to the shop and back again. Mind my manners and not to speak with anyone. If I was asked questions I was to let Bella answer them. We returned from the shop, I had a 10 pence mix up for me and five white chocolate mice for Tommy. Bella had treated us, telling me to choose a treat for us both as she was paying the shop owner for her cigarettes and milk. I ran up the two flights of stairs to show mum. I was starting to enjoy living in this house. We would spend time watching movies, doing jigsaws and I was now allowed to make the mums a cup of tea. I wasn't allowed to touch the hot kettle or be near the cooker when any of the ladies were cooking. All the rules of the house had to be adhered to as set out by

Bella on the day after our late night arrival. Mum, Bella, me and Selina had been sat around the kitchen table the following afternoon. Selina had a note pad and lots of leaflets she gave to mum. Papers for mum to sign and a colouring book and crayons she gave to me, 'a gift for being such a good girl' she said. I wasn't sure what I had done to deserve the gift but accepted it with grace, thanking her in a quiet voice, then being told to use my manners by mum who obviously hadn't heard me. "Hey, hey, she did use her manners, she's just a little shy at the minute, aren't you?" Selina said to me. I liked Selina, she wore a Puma T-shirt, blue jeans and a pair of umbro blue and white trainers. She had short dark hair cut in a boy's hair style, I thought. She had a very squeaky voice, didn't wear any make up but did have three gold necklaces around her neck and a gold ring or two on every finger. She had very blue eyes and very dark long eye lashes. "Anything you need, anything you want to ask, let me know, I cover three women's homes, so I'm here on and off, but if you need me at any time, just ask Bella to get hold of me and I will come round as soon as I can". Selina, then spent time talking to mum about solicitors, courts and injunctions. I started to colour in the book she had given me, I was colouring a princess dress in pink, shoes in yellow to represent gold and brown for the hair. Selina, mum and Bella were talking for a long time. I was starting to get hungry and asked mum what we were having for tea. Mum looked over in a stern voice, she told me to be quiet and not to interrupt when adults were talking. I looked down to the colouring book again. "Heyyyy, don't look so worried, you can say what you want when you want here love, no one has to be quiet and if you need to ask a question, don't save it up, you come right out and ask. Don't mind mummy, she's just a little tired, you had a busy night last night didn't you?" she said. I looked to mum who then looked at me and gave me a half smile. She looked very nervous and then looked back to her cup of tea, lifting it to her mouth to realise this was now empty. I stood up, pushing the chair with my legs along the floor which made a long loud screeching noise, that caused all three adults to wince and then hold their hands over their ears. "Oh Eddy, get up properly will you, don't push the chair like that", said mum. I stood looking at Selina who had a smile on her face. I sneaked a smile back at her when I thought mum wasn't looking. That smile confirmed my opinion of Selina, I liked her, she made me feel nice and she had brought me a gift that I hadn't earned and she didn't even know me. I was sold, we would be friends, I was sure of it. With spring in my step I walked over to the kitchen side where the kettle was set. "Ok, what do you want?" I asked them all. Selina, Bella and mum all looked over at me. Selina stood and walked over to me, "Hey no children allowed to touch any appliances in here, house rules, we don't want you burning yourself now do we?" she said. Mum's face turned scarlet red. "What has come over you Eddy, what would make you think you would be allowed to touch a dangerous hot kettle? You're not allowed to do it at home, so why do you think you can do it here?" she said. Before I could respond, she said, "Kids, you can't leave them for a minute before they start to think they are all grown up. None of the kids are allowed in the kitchen when I'm cooking let alone touch any of the appliances. She's just nervous and wants something to do don't you love?" she said to me. Her face still red and her eyes glaring at me. I stood in silence listening to her talking to Selina and Bella. Why would she be telling them lies? What had I done wrong? I was confused and could feel my heart beating in my ears. I was in trouble now, I could sense it. I looked up at Selina who was now stood right next to me and had taken the kettle from my hands. "Ok, I will make a brew for us all, do you want one Eddy? Can you help me? Can you get me another cup out of that cupboard over by the sink? Mummy can pass us the cups we have been using and then while the kettle is boiling you can tell me about your picture. I did as I was told and got the cup out of the cupboard. I sat back in the chair and showed Selina the princess I had coloured in. Selina was impressed with my colouring in. She found another page of a pony and rabbit in a field and asked if I would colour this in for her. She said she would leave that with me and if I wouldn't mind she would like to take that picture once complete to take home and put on her fridge. I nodded and agreed to do the picture for her fridge. We saw Selina again for a few minutes the following day. I was sitting on the sofa watching TV with Tommy. Mum had been talking to Bella sitting at the kitchen table and I was told to go and watch TV instead of sitting listening to adults talking. "Little pigs have big ears", said Bella as I was sat listening to her telling mum about when a husband had found the house and come round, banging on the door and threatening to set the house on fire if his wife didn't go outside to talk to him. She said the police arrived and arrested the husband then the emergency doctor had been called to give the lady valium to calm her nerves as she was in a right state after hearing his voice. I took in a gasp of air which alerted them to my presence. I was quickly ushered into the front room with Tommy. Selina walked past the door and bobbed her head round to say hello. She was a happy lady and I instantly felt calm just seeing her. "Hi Eddy, you still working on that picture for me?" she said. I nodded to her. As quick as she arrived at the door she was gone. I was getting used to the house, the ladies and baby Tommy. I had found a little blond haired baby doll in a plastic box behind the sofa. The box had some old small baby clothes at the bottom and some little socks. Is asked Bella who the doll belonged to. I was concerned it may have been left behind by another little girl who would be missing it. "Oh you mean 'Betty' said Bella. "She lives here, she's in need of a good wash and her hair brushing" she said. "Do you think you could do that for me and take care of her for me? I'm a little busy at the minute and don't have two minutes to sort her out. You would be doing me a big favour if you could make sure she is clean and put some clothes on her. I think one of the other children who lived here before forgot to dress her properly before they went to stay in their new home". I nodded my agreement and the deal was done. I would look after Betty and take care of her whilst I was here. I couldn't wait until it was our turn to move out to our new home. I took Betty to my room that night. Mum asked where I got the doll from. "Make sure you put that back in the morning, do you hear me?" I told mum about my chat with Bella and how I had agreed to look after Betty until we moved to out. Mum sat on the edge of the bed taking off her tights. She rolled them down her legs to her feet, one leg at a time. She pulled them off her feet and then set them on the little table near the door. "Once I get the family allowance for you sorted and find out how many points we have on the council waiting list, we should know how long we will have to wait until we get a choice of houses. The three areas I have put down should be great for us if we get one. The only trouble is, I had to ask for a three bedroomed house so we can get Lucy and the boys". I was excited about getting our new house, starting again without him. No more fear, no more threats, no more arguments. She sat back on the bottom of the bed, not saying anything, just sitting staring into space. I was also sat daydreaming; about the life we would have. I would be able to choose a new bedding, new clothes, we could stay up late on weekends and watch Opportunity Knocks without him turning the TV over. He didn't like Opportunity Knocks or the programs we all enjoyed. The only time we could watch this was when he had gone to the pub with his friends or hadn't come home from the pub. It was going to be so good, we were going to be so happy. I came back to the room when mum stood up and began to take off her dress by pulling it, over her head. She was tugging away at the dress trying to get it off her head but the dress wasn't moving. She looked so funny, stumbling around the room with her knickers and bra on, bare feet and her arms and head lost in the dress. I started to giggle at the sight. Mum also started to laugh, "I can't get the bloody thing off, Eddy help me," she said. She stumbled over to the bed. I stood up and walked from the head of the bed to the bottom, still giggling at the scene before me. I had just about managed to undo the top button for her to pull the dress over her head. She sat on the bottom of the bed still laughing at her mistake. I felt a tear build in my eyes, I hadn't heard this sound for such a long time. My heart was swelling with the happiness and relaxed feeling I was now getting used to. I was quite enjoying living in this house now. I was loved spending time alone, just me and mum, sitting in bed at night talking about what we would be able to do in our new house. The colours she would choose to decorate the lounge and kitchen. She had planned to get a grant from the council to pay for the emergency appliances. With the help from friends, we would soon have a nice fresh new looking house of our own. No longer having one cupboard to keep our food in our shelf in the fridge. I entered the small room to find mum with the drawers open and carrier bags on the bed with clothes in. She jumped as I burst into the room. She came over to the door in a rushed manner, pushed me into the room and closed the door quickly behind me. She put her index finger to her lips to shush me. "Look what Bella bought me from the shop", I said to her. She just hushed me and with her hands still holding onto my shoulders, she guided me to sit on the bottom of our bed. "Listen, I need to you to be very quiet and listen to me, we are going for a walk to the launderette in about half hour and I need you to come and help me. We can get a drink from the shop too once we have put the washing in the machine", she said. "Oh, can we get vimto?" I said. I stood up and walked towards the door, "Where are you going? Haven't I just told you we are going out?" she said. She gave me a bag and told me to put my coat on. I had just been out with Bella and didn't need my coat. It was warm outside and the launderette was only on the next street. "I don't want my coat, mum, it's warm outside". "Just put it on will you, they forecast rain for this afternoon and I don't want you to be getting cold" she said. I stopped at the door and took my coat off the hook on the back of the door. "Where are your navy tights?" she said. I just looked at her and shrugged, "dunno," I said. "Well you should know, I've told you before you need to look after your things". I put my hand on the door handle and turned the knob to go and look in the kitchen for my tights, they may be on the clothes maiden. "Where are you going? Shut that bloody door will you. I'm not ready yet, just hang on, we don't have to tell the whole bloody house when we are going out" she said. I stood near the door, looking at her. Was she angry with me? What had I done to make her angry? I had been a good girl all day, all week as far as I could remember. I hadn't wet the bed once whilst staying here. I had eaten all my dinner and hadn't been cheeky to anyone. She was now looking at me from the other side of the room. "Well don't just stand there, come and help me sort the washing bags". We didn't have many clothes, just two sets each. The ones we were wearing and the ones she had put into the bags. We did have three pairs of knickers each though, mum had gone and bought them with the money she got from the social three days after moving into the house. Mum must have been planning to do all the washing at once to save money, I thought. Once we had everything in the bags she walked towards me standing near the door. She stopped, looked around the room and then nodded her head for me to open the door, so we could go to the launderette and then to the shop to get some vimto. I set off out of the room and mum put her hand on my shoulder and then walked past me to get in front of me on the stairs. We got to the bottom of the stairs and I could hear the TV on in the lounge, it was the tea time news. As we reached the front door, I heard Tommy crying and Bella, saying "Ok, ok" but Tommy's cries went louder and Bella raised her voice, "Hold on a minute", she said, in a deep, urgent manner. I stopped and stood still, did she want us to get anything from the shop for her? Did she want us to get her some vimto too? Mum grabbed my arm and pulled me towards her and out of the front door. I was startled and looked at her then just as I was about to ask, what was wrong. She put her index finger to my lips again and waved her hand, for me to hurry down the path. She turned right out of the garden gate and down the street and I followed her, running trying to keep up with her fast walking pace. "Come on, will ya, we need to be quick, I don't want any of those nosey bleeders following me" she said. We turned left at the end of the street and then she slowed down a little, walking at a fast pace, in a hurried manner. We passed the newsagents and bakery before we reached the launderette. We walked through the door, into the empty and silent launderette, which had a strong smell of tobacco smoke and detergent mixed together. A long wooden bench stood down the middle, covered in graffiti and carved-out names. Large washing machines filled one wall and drying machines filled the opposite wall with a single silver metal spinning machine at the end of the row. There was another door at the other end of the launderette with a STAFF sign marked above it. The door was also covered in colourful graffiti. She dropped the bags on the floor and sat on the bench. She let out a long sigh. I walked over to one of the machines in the middle of the room, I looked in through the dark large round window. I leaned my head on the window. Then turned to face mum. She was striking a match and lighting a cigarette, still sitting on the bench, looking directly out of the window, watching as people walked past the large window. Can I put the money in the machine? Can I mum? Which one are we using? Can we just choose any? Do you want me to put the clothes in the machine?" I said walking towards her with the intention of taking the clothes out of the bag to put them in the machine. "Oh for god's sake Eddy give it a rest will you? I'm not doing any bloody washing. We barely have two pennies to rub together, how the hell do you think I'm going to be able to afford to throw money away in one of those bleeding machines? We can wash the clothes when..." she stopped speaking mid-sentence. I was looking over at her, confused. I stood up trying to make sense of the situation. She had said that's why we were here. What's up with her? Was she getting upset again. She had been very different in the last two days. I thought she was starting to feel happy, she had been in a better mood. She hadn't cried herself to sleep for the past two nights. She had smiled and let me sit with my head leaning on her when we were watching a movie last night and then went to bed with me instead of sitting up with the other mothers chatting, smoking cigarette and drinking tea. She looked different now, nervous and her hands were shaking as she put the cigarette up to her mouth. She was getting sad again, I was sure of it. I walked back over to the washing machines and breathed on the glass to steam this up and then I could draw a picture of our new happy home with a chimney and smoke coming from it. Mum was sitting still looking out of the window, not doing the washing, just staring into space. I had rubbed over the picture of our new house and was then breathing on the glass again and written my name. I rubbed the glass again and looked at the window as a car light shone in through the window, lighting the launderette up, highlighting how dirty and old the shop was. Mum was still sitting with the bags beside her on the floor. Why did we have our knickers and all of our own clothes in the bags if she didn't have two pennies to rub together and wash our clothes? Why were we in here? I daren't ask her though, she was upset again, I knew it. I was now walking past each washing machine, running my hands across the glass doors, looking in each one. Then I heard the door to the launderette opened. I turned my head to look at the door and see who else was coming to do washing or even drying. My body became fixed to the spot, my hand still stretched out touching the window of the washing machine. Was I dreaming, or was I having a nightmare. Wake up, wake up I was saying in my head. As I chanted Wake up, Wake up, quickly, wake up, in my head. I felt the blood draining from my face and my heart start to beat loudly, my legs were feeling weak. My vision fixed on the door as the large, dark silhouette of a man stepped in through the door. I felt the nausea building in my throat, my legs getting weaker, but an overwhelming feeling of being stuck to the spot. It was him, he had entered my dreams, no matter how far away we fled, or how long we stayed away, he would find me in my dreams. NO, NO, NO, I won't believe this, I can't believe she would do this. Not after all she had said, all the promises she had made. What about OUR house? The one where we could go to bed at night without fear of being woken by arguing. He's found us, I thought. What do we do now? Do we run? Is there anywhere to hide? Should I scream, would anyone hear my screams. I inhaled, ready to let out the loudest scream ever to alert someone, anyone. Let them know we were in danger, he had found us, what was he going to do to us? My heart was beating faster and faster in my chest, my bladder twitching now with nerves. I quickly dashed to mums side, I crouched at the side of the bench and sat back on my heels to stop myself from peeing. I couldn't stand and prevent the urine from escaping my bladder. I had not had this feeling since the night we left our home. I had continued to have dry nights whilst staying in the small bed with mum. Why was my body failing me now? We needed to run, I needed strength in my legs to get away. We were here alone with no one to protect us. Bella said we were safe, she had said he would not find us. She was wrong, he had found us. Tears started to run down my face and urine trickle down my shoes. Just as I was about to let out the air from my lungs to scream. He spoke, "You ok Love?" he said as he looked directly at mum. "You been waiting long? Got everything?" he said. My whole body started to shake, I couldn't stop it. I had completely wet myself, tears rolling down my face, sobbing in a squatting position, I just looked on in shock. What did he mean? *Waiting Long, Got Everything?* It didn't take long for the realisation of the situation to darn on me. She knew he would be coming here. She had planned this, had arranged for him to meet her here. She must have told him where we were. I looked behind him, to see if he was alone. I expected Lucy and the boys to come in behind him, but no, he was alone. Mum stood up as he walked towards her, she stood up picked up the bags of washing and walked towards him with her head down. I had by now lowered myself to the floor, sitting in a puddle of urine, still crying. The fear and disappointment encompassing my whole being. He didn't look in my direction, just took the bags from her and turned to face the door, standing by her, he put his free arm around her shoulder, leaned in and kissed her on top of her head. She leaned into him and tilted her head into his chest. "We can sort this, together" he said. They reached the door and stopped. He leaned down and spoke quietly into her head. Then he turned around, threw one of the bags of clothes over to me, "Get changed into some clean clothes and don't take all day. Some things will never change, hey, pissy arse" he said. Together they walked out of the launderette, leaving me sitting in the puddle on the floor, now sobbing, unable to control my grief. The launderette seemed such a large cold room now. My legs still feeling weak and still unable to control my breathing, I stood up using the bench to lever myself into a standing position. I untucked my T-shirt to cover my modesty. I found some clean knickers and some boy's shorts Bella had given me. I was just tucking my Tshirt into the shorts when the door opened again. He stood with the door open and shouted, "Stop pissing about and come get into the car, we're not waiting all bleeding night for you". I jumped from the spot and grabbed the bag and wet clothes to my chest and rushed to the door. As I got to the door to walk past him my heart began to pound even louder and harder against my chest. I was still in disbelief he had found us. I felt my whole world was crumbling in front of my eyes. As I walked past him at the door, I felt the heat of his slap on the back of my head. "Come on, for Christ sake, don't push your luck, pissy arse, get in the car, I don't have all night to wait for you. It'd be all the same to me if I left you here, but your mum won't have that, SO MOVE IT", he shouted. I climbed the step into the back of the Bedford van, he slammed the doors shut behind me. I was sat on one of the benches, holding onto the makeshift seat, trying to prevent myself from falling as he turned corners. Watching the shops and houses of our 'safe' neighbourhood, as we left them behind. "I'm warning you now. If you don't shut that bleeding snivelling, I'll give you something to snivel about", he said. I held my breath in an attempt to stop the tears.